BILL'S MAGIC BOX

ISBN 979-8-8496268-8-8

Bill's Magic Box LLC
PO Box 6782
Denver, CO
80206

BILL'S MAGIC BOX
STORIES FOR CHILDREN

R.C. Hammond

Introduction

Once upon a time I was cleaning my garage when I came across an old box. Painted on the front of the box was the word *Bills*. My thought was that it was once used to hold bills, like water or electric bills.

It was a nice old box, so I took it inside and was about to set it down when I saw a punctuation that I must have missed. It was an apostrophe. The box now read, *Bill's*. This, of course, changed the meaning. The box must have belonged to a *Bill*. But I didn't know any *Bills*, and there weren't any *Bills* in my family, past or present.

I didn't think much of it until the next day when the box caught my eye and I saw more words written on the box. *Bill's Magic Box* was now what it read.

Ok, was I losing my mind? I was fairly certain - though my eyes are bad and I'm old - I didn't see those words on the box before. Not only that - there was something in it! (I knew it was empty before! I'm not that old!)

Inside of the box were gold papers tied with a red silk ribbon. Written on the papers was a story. A children's rhyming story, to be more precise.

I read the story, put it back in the box, shut the lid, rose out of my chair, and backed away slowly. What was happening was very strange.

It took me some time to muster up the courage to open the box again. When I did, there was the roll of gold papers tied with the red ribbon. I was sure that when I tossed the story back in the box I didn't roll it up and tie it with the ribbon. But there it was - rolled up and tied.

I took a deep breath, untied the ribbon, and read. And yes! Of course! *It was a different story!*

So what do I do? What *could* I do? I feel I have no choice but to share my findings.

These are the stories found in *Bill's Magic Box*. I hope you enjoy them.

Your Friend,

R.C.

The Top

Here's the thing about being a top:

I don't know when I'll spin,

I don't know when I'll stop.

I'm not sure if you can quite understand

what it's like to be at the mercy

of little human hands.

Most days I lie in wait and wonder

will I be found by want or blunder?

Will I be picked up and spun to be twirled in glee?

Or will a foot accidentally step on me?

Will I be dropped in a bin, or kicked to the side,

or left under a seat during a family car ride?

There must be some type of a connection

between my life of random direction

and being made from wood, just for fun,

by an old man for his great grandson.

An old woodworker with time to spare

with wrinkled hands and frosty hair;

with scraps of wood, and rusty tools,

and an old workbench shaped like a spool.

I was thought of one evening, and made that same night,

and by dawn's day spinning under a candlelight

to the smile of the old man and his thoughts of his gift

to his great grandson and the spirits I'd lift.

Those first small hands were the best I suppose

as he spun me, and spun me, and smiled at me close.

This was back in medieval days

when the hills were covered in a misty haze.

No phones or computers into which to stare,

no sounds of motors filling the air;

when toys with batteries didn't exist

and toys like me were the greatest gift.

And though I'm old, ancient in fact,

all my parts are still intact.

I have my shoulder, my body, and my tip,

and a round dowel crown for fingers to grip.

My shoulder is made of hickory,

my body made of peach,

my tip a dark mahogany,

my crown a purple teak.

And though I have some nicks, and scratches,

dents, and bruises, and soiled patches,

I can still spin with the best of them.

Them being whatever tops are *in*.

But I'm afraid these days if you're a top

in wouldn't be a name someone would drop

on a simple toy that's made of wood.

I'd spin back in time if I could.

Which brings me to my point,

back to my problem,

and why I speak these words

hoping you'll solve them.

All I want to do is twirl.

Twirl, and twirl, and twirl, and TWIRL!

I want two little fingers to give me a spin

so I spin, and spin, and spin, and SPIN!

I want to spin forever and EVER!

But that's just not my life, I've come to discover.

Imagine an astronaut being stuck on the ground.

Imagine a king who lost his crown.

Imagine a balloon without any air.

That's right, my life, it just isn't fair.

I bet you can see, and hear, and taste

without needing someone to rearrange your face.

Can you walk on your own, hop, skip, or jump

without getting a nudge, a push, or a bump?

I wonder if you appreciate the freedom

to run and play whenever you're needin';

to roll on the ground, or swing on a swing,

jump in a lake, or laugh, or sing.

I have no such freedoms, no not at all.

There's no one I can talk to, no one to call.

It seems my days have become mundane

as I lie in wait for someone to say,

'Hey! Look! It's a top! What a well-made toy!

I think I'll give it a spin! Oh what joy!'

But I'm afraid such days might be gone for a while

as I sit in a dump on a large garbage pile.

I was thrown away not by accident

when a long day her parents spent

cleaning her room and getting rid of her stuff,

and all the toys she had played with enough.

At their garage sale I had no buyers,

only the electronics would the children admire.

(By the end of the day I even had a note that read *FREE*!)

So into the garbage her parents sent me.

Well I've been in tough spots throughout my life

and this is just another.

I was tossed out of a window one time

and spent countless days in a gutter.

I went down in the sea on a pirate's ship.

I was taken across country on a cowboy's hip.

In 1812 I took part in a war

when a cannonball went through my playmate's floor.

With his parents from his house he fled.

Instead of me, he took his buck knife instead.

I've sat in a cellar for a century.

Had a child bury me.

Forgotten in many closets and if I had tears

I would have cried them dry from all the years

I've spent alone,

all by myself,

sometimes for all to see

me sitting,

not spinning,

on a shelf.

But I know time will pass as it always does,

and if time is a poison I'm aware of the cause.

It's because I'm just a top

and time for me will never stop.

(It hasn't yet.)

And I'm willing to bet

that I'll never be broken.

(I haven't been yet.)

The reason is this:

it was how I was made,

with loving thoughts

when I was created.

I remember quite well those calloused, wrinkled hands

and the time it took, and the patience he had.

So I know I'll outlive my lonely days

and once again be part of a craze,

a fad, or a movement, if you will,

when tops once again are king of the hill.

It might take time for this to happen,

a year, a century, or perhaps a millennium.

And I don't know how long I'll remain stationary

on a world that spins in a circle, on its axis, daily.

But maybe the next time you come upon a top

it would be nice if you would come to a stop

and think about the life it's leading

not spinning, motionless, in needing.

Take a moment, stoop to the ground,

put it between your fingers, spin it around!

For if you do this wonderful deed

perhaps one day when you're in need -

a day when you're feeling all alone,

down in the dumps in an empty home,

forlorn, and lost, and all but forgotten,

depressed, and sad, and feeling rotten

you'll remember looking down, and coming to a stop,

and finding on the ground a lonely top.

You'll remember giving that top a spin,

and you'll remember how it made you grin.

And maybe, just maybe, as your having this thought

suddenly you'll hear a knock,

and when you open your front door

a bunch of kids will be on your porch

smiling, and happy, all joining in to say,

'Hey!

Do you wanna come out and play?'

Tag

'Tag! You're it!' was what I heard first

as a stranger touched me and then took off in a burst.

There was screaming and scattering in all degrees

with everyone running away from me.

So there in wonder and shock I stood

trying to think as hard as I could,

Tag? What is that? And why am I *it*?

What was going on I hadn't a clue

for this game of Tag I never pursued.

It was as if all the kids didn't want me to be

sharing in their reverie.

It was as if they had all singled me out,

and just to let me know, began to shout,

'You're it!' 'You're it!'

'You can't catch me!'

I don't know if you've ever been in my shoes

where others created a game for you to lose.

And I don't know if you've ever been in my position

where others ran away from you like you were poison.

And I don't know if you've ever been in my spot

where others looked at you like you were rot.

But maybe there has been a time you've been

stuck in a game you can never win.

'You're it!' 'You're it!'

'You'll always be it!'

Well the longer I stood there the more painful it was,

my thoughts spinning in circles, my head all abuzz.

I knew I had to do something, I had to think fast,

I didn't want this attention to last.

By now everyone at me was staring,

at me they were shouting,

at me they were daring,

'You can't catch me!'

11

'You can't catch me!'

I think there's something you should all know:

to this event I didn't want to go.

A party my parents dragged me into

'kicking and screaming' as it's been referred to.

The only people I knew were all very old,

and when it came to the children I knew not a soul.

'You're it!' 'You're it!'

'You'll always be it!'

Clearly they all knew one another,

they were all cousins, or friends, sisters, or brothers.

And by the simple fact they all knew what to do,

pointing and shouting as around me they flew,

it seemed to me that they all knew how to play

this game of Tag since their very first day.

They've been playing this game since they were born!

Of this I was certain, of this I was sure.

'You can't catch me!'

'You'll always be it!'

The racket was getting hard on my ears -

the shouting, the yelling, the taunts, and the jeers.

So I bounced on my toes, and spun around,

and pretended to duck into the crowd.

I guess that's what was supposed to happen

because a few kids broke into laughing.

Others screamed and ran away,

and that's when it became

clear as day:

the reason I was *it*

and why the game became legit

was because someone *tagged* me

and shouted, *'You're it!'*

So off I launched to the nearest bunch

who I thought were having a particular hunch

that I really knew not what to do,

so off I took and toward them I flew.

13

With looks of fear, and looks of surprise,

they began to realize

that maybe I did know how to play this game,

and one of them I was about to shame.

Or at least that's what I wanted them to think

as I picked out the loudest in the rink.

'You're it! You're it!

You'll always be it!'

I decided to pick the loudest.

I decided to chase the proudest.

I'd go after the one who never lost

and tag him first

whatever the cost.

'You can't catch me!

You'll always be it!'

I didn't run after him right away

because now it was my turn to play

my own game, in my own mind,

and I'd take my own leisurely time.

I ran this-way-and-that pretending to chase

the slowest child in the race,

while out of the corner of my eye

I drew a close bead on my prize -

the one who was shouting the most defiant,

'You'll never catch anybody!

You'll always be it!'

I heard him make fun of me and call me bad names,

things not nice to say to someone new to a game.

So I slowed my pace, and pretended I was tired,

and put on a look of sadness like I might retire

away from the game and quit.

'You can't quit now,' he said. *'You're it!'*

It was clear that he was the leader of these kids

because they all repeated what he just said.

'Yeah!' 'You can't quit!' 'You're it!'

I tried my best to bring tears to my eyes,

I did my best to keep my disguise.

I put my head down, and came to a stop,

and all the kids did what I had thought.

They came closer to me with the loudest in front.

They came closer to me with him leading the taunt,

'You're it! You'll always be it!

You can't catch anybody! Quitter!'

That's when I jumped because I knew he wasn't ready!

On my feet I was nimble and steady

and in one bounding leap

for him I did reach

hoping my lesson would spread and teach

to all those kids that being the newest

doesn't mean that you're the stupidest!

I touched him quickly and off I did sprint

yelling,

'Tag!

You're it!'

The Coolest Puppy

There was a fancy puppy

who had a shiny coat,

he had the nicest collars,

an airplane, and a boat.

His doghouses were multi-storied

but he didn't sleep in them,

high-rises and penthouses

was where his time was spent.

Dog bowls made of solid gold

of those he had plenty.

In the evening he slept on blankets

a pharaoh would even envy.

It just so happened

he was the rarest breed,

a cross between a Bulldog,

Great Dane, and a Pekinese.

He had a little bit of shepherd,

a little bit of hound,

a little bit of wiener dog,

the lowest to the ground.

His fur felt like the finest linens,

his eyes a crystal green,

his toenails were made of rhino horn,

as odd as that may seem.

His teeth they glistened like Akoya pearls,

at the end of his tail rolled perfect curls.

He was the handsomest, classiest,

puppy around

and all the puppies knew him

in all the doggy-show towns.

Looking at the pyramid

of the world's most popular pups,

he would be at the capstone,

the very tippy top.

As far as famous canines

no dog even came close,

not even Scooby-Doo

who was always chased by ghosts.

More famous he was than Lassie, or Snoopy,

Rin Tin Tin, Toto,

Comet, or Goofy.

Laika was the first dog sent into space.

Old Yeller brought tears to everyone's face.

Benji and Air Bud were stars of the screen…

But our puppy was cooler,

not to be mean.

There wasn't a dog show he didn't win

blue ribbons and trophies in every event he was in.

His leashes were woven with the finest threads,

and only by the finest would he be led.

Astronauts, artists, nobles of the court,

all the famous athletes of all the greatest sports,

presidents, dictators, generals, and majors,

producers and musicians who owned their own labels,

monks, squires, earls, and deans -

with the Coolest Puppy

they'd all want to be seen.

Now you'd think that being the Coolest Puppy

would be pretty keen

and having everything you ever wanted

would be a puppy's dream.

But there was one thing the Coolest Puppy

never ever had,

and the more he lacked this very thing

the more it made him sad.

As the trophies stacked up on the shelves

and the blue ribbons piled high,

the Coolest Puppy was losing that sparkle,

that twinkle in his eye.

He started to slink, he started to shuffle,

he began to mope about.

He was losing his mojo, his style,

that cool, suave puppy clout.

His curls began to knot,

his coat to lose its shine.

All the Coolest Puppy wanted to do

was sleep all the time.

Day by day and week by week

he was dropping out of the hype,

missing all the doggie shows

as they went traveling by.

His jets remained in their hangars,

his yachts along their berths,

he was becoming the saddest puppy

that ever roamed the earth.

One by one his people left him

going their own way,

they didn't want to be seen with a puppy

getting sadder by the day.

One might believe that the Coolest Puppy

could make the personal change

to rid himself of the problem

that was making him feel so strange.

But the Coolest Puppy he really didn't know

why he was feeling so low.

He had no idea,

not a clue,

why he was feeling so blue.

And as sadness brings sadness as sadness does,

the saddest puppy forgot about

his ritzy life that was.

The glitz, the glamour, the fortune, and fame;

all the Sunset billboards flashing his sparkling name;

the radio, the television, the internet shows;

people asking for autographs

wherever he did go.

All that vanished, went kaput, completely disappeared,

and for the Coolest Puppy

no one seemed to care.

But his sadness kept growing

and still he knew not why

while he spent his lonely days

with tears upon his eyes.

Dirty and forgotten, covered in soot and ash,

he'd often spend his nights

sleeping in piles of trash.

Then there came one rainy night

in a back alley's puddled blight

when he was stinky, and smelly, and soaking wet,

and wondering why his life wasn't done yet,

from out of the darkness and out of the gloom

a tiny silhouette before him did loom.

As it came close a small figure appeared

along with a crying

hardly audible to his ears.

It was a little kitty, lost and alone,

the tiniest little kitty who didn't have a home.

She was limping, and whimpering, and how sad it was.

How could this happen and what was the cause?

So cold and so wet the tiny kitty looked

that even the Saddest Puppy's heart was shook.

'Excuse me,' our Saddest Puppy managed to say.

(It had been a long time

since he used his voice that way.)

'I see that you're sad, even sadder than I,

and alone, and forgotten, and I'm wondering why?

For such a tiny kitty this shouldn't be so,

please tell me how your life did go.

You can curl up beside me and tell me your tale,

for your fur is mangy and look at your tail

it's broken and crooked you poor little thing.

How did this happen? What fate did life bring?'

But she didn't understand,

she spoke no doggy tongue,

and even if she did

no good it would have done.

For the poor little kitty had no voice to speak,

when she tried to talk it was only a squeak.

The poor little kitty into a life she was born

parked in a lot in a thunderstorm,

placed in a box in a shopping cart.

She had nothing,

nothing at all,

from the very start.

That night the Saddest Puppy

kept her as warm as he could,

but the next day he had to tell her

as he thought he should,

'Listen, tiny kitty, here's the thing,

I have nothing for you, nothing to bring.

No food, no milk, no roof over my head.

You should find someone else to be with instead.'

But the little kitty just stared at him

understanding not a word,

she looked at him, and smiled,

and let out a little purr.

So the Saddest Puppy became more demanding.

'Go on, go away, find another place to stay!'

But instead of leaving, she started to play.

She jumped on his head, and licked his ear,

bounced down his body, and bit his rear.

She pounced and wrestled until he barked, 'Stop!

You don't get it!

I can't be your friend!

All this happiness, it must end!'

But it was clear to the Saddest Puppy

that she didn't understand,

so he decided to take matters into his own hands.

He snuck away in the middle of the night,

and he was alone once again by next day's light.

'It was for her own good,' he grumbled to himself.

'My life is so sad I could never help

that poor little creature so small and so frail

with her mangy fur and broken tail;

with her poor little voice that can't even speak

and nothing comes out but only a peep.'

So again the Saddest Puppy

wandered alone

day after day

all on his own.

If you saw him in the city

you'd have to take pity.

If you saw him in your town

you'd have to frown.

People wanted to help him

but at them he just growled.

His demeanor, his ways, his manners

had become oh so foul.

So people stayed away,

he wanted no one's help,

and aimlessly he wandered

talking to himself.

And then one day when he was slouched on a bench

a girl sat down beside him

and began to eat her lunch.

She had a shiny white dress

and curly red hair.

All our Saddest Puppy did

was look ahead and stare.

'Do you want some of my sandwich?' she asked,

but he just growled and *grrr*-ed.

'My,' the curly-haired girl did say,

'those are the rudest words

I think I've ever heard.'

'*Grrr,*' said the Saddest Puppy, 'it just isn't fair.

How can anybody let her walk around

with bugs in her hair?

She has nothing, nothing at all,

and she's so very small.

I don't understand it,

I don't understand it at all

how the world can be so cruel,

so mean, and disrespectful.'

'On whom are you taking pity?'

asked the curious girl.

'I'm talking about a kitty,'

the Saddest Puppy snarled.

'*Kitties?* I love kitties!'

the girl said swinging her feet.

'If I had a kitty I'd hug it, and hold it,

and give it lots of treats!'

The Saddest Puppy sat up straight

as if he had won a prize.

That something he was missing from his life

he suddenly did realize!

Off our newfound dog did sprint,

and the little girl watched him

with a shrug and a squint.

So now we cut to a later time,

years have passed on down the line.

We find ourselves in front of a stage

in a theatre made famous because of its age.

On the pedestal,

the podium if you will,

from under a tuxedo

swings a broken tail.

There stands a cat with a conductor's baton

doing something that's never been done.

The first cat ever to direct a symphony show

with a hundred-piece orchestra sitting below.

The only cat in the world

to compose a masterpiece

and perform it to a sold-out crowd

with glamour, poise, and grace.

And when she's done

she'll take a bow

to the audience clapping and whistling loud.

Her curly-haired owner will be smiling proud

from her gilded box seat above the crowd.

And far in the back,

in the farthest seat,

a dog in the shadows is on his feet.

He's wearing a fancy hat,

and mirrored sunglasses,

a shiny velvet suit,

and shoes with silver laces.

He has a sparkle in his eye, and he's nodding with a grin,

thinking of the kitty, and where her life has been.

He'll slide out the back, after the show,

and no one will even notice.

For as far as puppies go,

our puppy's still the coolest.

THE DANCE OF THE MCSNEEDS

I want to tell you how to be just like me -

happy, and joyful, and forever free!

I have no cares in the world, no bad thoughts in my mind!

I just dance, and play, and create my time!

I bounce around colors, and prance in the light,

twirl, and spin in a wonderful life!

No one is happier!

No sirree!

But it wasn't always like this…

No…

not for me.

I was born into the worst world there ever could be,

and as I share this tale I'm sure you'll agree.

Talk about horrors, the fear, and the greed,

let me introduce you to Mr. Doogle McSneed.

He owned my world, everything I could see,

and I worked day and night fulfilling his needs.

Imagine a world of endless parts

where everything looks recently taken apart.

Nothing quite fits, and nothing quite works,

all is designed to keep me in work.

Whoa, what a mess, that world of mine

where I had to fix everything right on time.

McSneed would yell, 'My toffee young man!

I want it now (*clap! clap!*) do you understand?'

But the toffee maker was made

in five different parts of the world,

and when I turned it on

it rumbled, and swirled,

grumbled, and clanked, and spat to a halt,

and if I got too close

I'd get quite a jolt!

So on to McSneed's Fixits to find the right part.

'Nope! We don't have it!' the clerk would bark.

So on to the next store, the next, and the next.

By the time I was done I had parts up to my neck!

But none of them fit, none of them connected,

and all my excuses Mr. Doogle McSneed rejected.

You see all the stores were owned by McSneed,

and everything was run by the family McSneed.

Brothers, and nephews, cousins, and aunts.

Grandpa McSneed managed the toffee parts plant.

The McSneeds were everywhere,

they ran my whole town.

I was the only non-McSneed around!

They laughed in my face, pushed me about,

told me I was a clown, stupid, a lout.

A horrible place I tell you it was

where my whole world was ruled from above.

So what did I do? How did I get free?

I'll tell you my secret so maybe you'll see.

I changed my mind! I changed my thoughts!

I decided I would readjust!

I thought about nothing but good things each day!

I wouldn't let bad things get in my way!

I decided to put love into every part I touched!

There would be absolutely *nothing*

I could love too much!

'Hello!' I said, smiling to Stanley McSneed.

'I need an F13X bolt to get toffee

to Mr. Doogle McSneed!'

'We don't have that part you ignorant toad!

Go see my brother, he's right down the road!'

But instead of feeling down, or stepped on, or hated,

I skipped down the street feeling free and elated!

I decided that nothing would hurt me, no, not ever.

Not McSneed, nor his needs, nor that un-oiled lever.

I loved everything, everything I saw

because it was my life, and my life was all!

I woke up each morning and clacked my heels,

rolled somersaults, and spun cartwheels!

'Hello, toffee maker! How are you today?

I bet you need fixing! I can't wait to play!'

Well that lever hit me like it did every day,

the spring popped out, the parts flew about,

it hissed, and spun, and coughed, and rattled.

But, oh, I loved that machine

when it made such a prattle!

'Where's my toffee!' McSneed would scream

while I was living my magical dream.

'Mr. McSneed,' I'd respond, in bouncy song,

'that toffee you want, well something went wrong!

That machine of yours does a funky dance!

Like this!' I'd jig. 'And like that!' I'd prance.

I'd imitate his machine as best I could

with dancing, and noises, moving however I should.

Mr. McSneed would look at me as if I'd lost my mind

as I danced around his office

having a glorious time.

'This is atrocious young man! You've lost your noggin!

You'll be fired, you understand,

and in the streets you'll be sloggin'!'

But did I care? No, not a whit!

In his face I laughed, and he had quite a fit!

He told me, 'Be gone, your time is done!

My town is no place for having fun!'

But it mattered not to me, I felt no care in the world,

and out of his office I pliéed with a whirl!

One day I was skipping and singing songs to myself

when I noticed there was no more food on the shelves.

All the McSneed businesses, they had come to a halt.

I wondered out loud, 'Could this be my fault?'

I realized right then who was keeping things going.

It was *I* who kept the McSneed town rolling!

I was the one who fixed all the stuff!

Without me, those McSneeds, they had it rough!

And then one day from out of the blue

McSneed called me with a different tune.

He told me he wanted me back.

But I told him without much tact,

'Who? *Me?*

I can't possibly work

for a greedy McSneed.'

'I'll pay you double,' his stomach gurgled.

'Triple in fact!'

'It's not about money,' I told him. 'You know that.'

Oh, how splendid it is, in a delightful way,

that all my problems have drifted away.

Sometimes I'll work, sometimes I'll sleep;

maybe I'll eat scones, or bathe my feet.

I don't think about it much, I'm too busy singing.

The future and past, I don't give much thinking.

The cycle was endless, I was stuck and caught,

until I decided to change my thoughts.

I'm the artist now… The Director… The Creator!

All the world is now my theatre!

'Action!' I shout and jump out of bed

with wonderful thoughts in my head!

I'll wear a raccoon cap, or put on superhero undies,

or spritz on a perfume that smells like ice cream sundaes!

Maybe I'll wear a cape, or a faux fur shawl,

or put on dizzying shoes that make me ten feet tall!

A musical it is, and I'm the singer and the dancer!

Yes, that's right, that's my answer!

And just to confirm that my feelings were right

a miracle occurred late one night.

That toffee maker started to spin and whir;

it whistled, and tooted, and hummed, and purred.

It started up and worked perfectly like never before,

and created perfect toffee for McSneed's perfect world!

A joyous sound it was, and I sang along,

and all night we danced singing our toffee-making song!

In fact, I haven't stopped, and it's been quite a thrill

as I skip, and hop, and whistle a trill.

I do the Toffee Machine Rumba!

And the Toffee Machine Samba!

I even made up my own dance

called the Toffee Machine Wambamba!

So hello, life, and all your non-fitting parts,

to McSneed, and his greed, the stops, and the starts.

Oh, how I love my world…

Gosh I'm clever…

I know I'll always be…

happy forever.

The Stairs

The stairs can be a scary place,

especially in a house that doesn't have much space.

With two of you running and setting the pace,

you don't want to hit the stairs during a race.

If you do you might find space scarce

when you hit the top of the stairs,

sprinting side by side,

when the stairs can only handle one at a time.

Something's gotta give,

somebody's gotta give up some room,

you can't be thinking the same thing

and singing the same tune.

Whether it's a friend, or brother,

sister, or some other,

racing down the stairs together

is going to lead to trouble.

If you both think you can make it down first

no doubt somebody's bound to get hurt.

And how do I know this?

How can I make such a claim?

Let's just say, I learned it the hard way.

I raced my brother once,

and if I had been smart, and not a dunce,

I would have let him go first and stepped back with pride.

Instead, I was being stupid inside.

I have to win was what I was thinking

because we were both trying to get to the kitchen.

Making it there first was quite a prize,

to yell, *'First!',* to Dad's smiling eyes.

It was a typical evening, we were watching TV,

when we heard Dad yell, 'Dinner's ready!'

we shot up to leave.

One of the problems with being the youngest,

and the smallest, and not the strongest,

is that I always have to sit on the floor

and never get the chair that's next to the door

that gives my brother the advantage

of being on his feet first.

Toward the door my brother burst.

Quick to react, I tripped his foot,

he stumbled hard and hit the wall good.

But he bounced off as if he were rubber

and gave me a shoulder that made me see double.

I hit the doorframe and saw a few stars,

but justice was served when he stepped on a car.

A toy that just happened to be in the right place.

'Ow!' he yelled with a grimacing face.

I laughed and gave him a push

into a hall table that held some books.

The table toppled, and to the floor it crashed,

spilling the books, and the drawer that was attached.

Well, we both knew we couldn't just leave

or we'd both be in trouble deep.

So as fast as we could

we picked up what we should,

he the books, I the drawer

and everything that was spilled on the floor.

(I have to say our effort was poor.

It sure didn't look like it did before.)

But he took off without a care

heading for the top of the stairs.

So I reached out and grabbed his collar

and he let out a bit of a holler

as I pulled back and jumped ahead.

That's when he pulled the hair on my head.

Now scratching, and poking, and punching

are forbidden,

and I'd add hair-pulling to that if it were my decision.

So together we both made it to the top of the stairs,

I, pulling his shirt; he, pulling my hair.

But we both knew we had to quit

running side by side because we just couldn't fit.

For our house is old

and there's a four-cornered mould

on top of a post

to stop any approach.

On the other side

there's a hard corner

and a wall.

Little did we know

we were headed for a fall.

I shoved him and he shoved me

changing both our trajectories.

I hit the post and he hit the corner -

it didn't take long

before we knew we were goners.

Our running hadn't slowed a bit

as we both lost our footing grip.

Built in the early 1900's, I was told,

our house is more than one hundred years old.

An old brick house that isn't forgiving,

but it's been mine since I started living.

So to live in a house with standards of safety

I wouldn't know what that meant even if you paid me.

Asbestos in the basement,

lead pipes under the floors,

dark square rooms separated

by splintered, paint-chipped doors.

And the wood stairs we were about to fall down

are hard, and narrow, and steep.

Even walking down slowly

one's balance is hard to keep.

Each step you take

needs some consideration,

and it's best to hold onto the railing

while keeping your concentration.

But such heedfulness neither of us had

as he slammed into the corner bad.

I took the post in a rib

and both of us slid…

We were going too fast…

We just couldn't stop…

So together we launched…

over the top.

Of course, before the steps, we could have let up

instead of hitting them at a full-on gallop.

We could have been smart and called the race a tie

instead of hitting the stairs side by side.

They say that hindsight is twenty-twenty

and I've come to agree with that statement plenty.

Our refusal to stop at the top of the stairs

launched us flailing into the air

above the hard wood in the dark narrow space

that was just about to end our race.

I wonder if my brother was thinking the same thing,

like the impossibility of making a soft landing.

As we were both in the air

looking down on the stairs,

our bodies behind us, faces first,

right then I was thinking

life couldn't be worse.

If you've ever found yourself in a terrible crash

you know the moment seems to last

forever and ever despite the commotion

as your brain takes it in

in super slow motion.

What happened next was all a blur,

I couldn't tell you what exactly occurred.

I kind of remember the lights of the ride

and sharing an ambulance side by side.

And our hospital beds at night

under blue fluorescent lights.

I had seven stitches; he had ten.

But I wouldn't consider that a win.

What it was, I believe, was another lesson

and every day I thank the heavens

that it didn't end up worse.

But do you think that lesson changed our course?

No!

We still race as fast as we can

to get to the kitchen first!

But things have changed.

Our minds have been trained.

We have a silent agreement

when we hit the top of the stairs.

(And as a reminder, both of our scars are still there.)

Sometimes he'll slow down

and let me go first.

Other times

(more than half of the time?)

stopping will be my choice.

For we remember the pain

and there's still a bloodstain

from when we raced down

mutually,

and we both agree

that it's better not to have our branches

missing from the family tree.

It's as if our old house

commanded some sort of respect

with its stairs that transfer

from one level to the next.

Yes, our old house has made it quite clear

that stairs are a mindful place.

They're not something you want to run down

even when you're in a race.

I'm Happy I'm Not A Loggerhead

Man, oh boy, I'm sure a lucky kid!

I just learned something that blew my lid!

The Loggerhead turtle, those poor little dudes,

what a life they're brought into

as basically food!

From people, to birds, to big fish in a feeding,

there's nothin' out there that probably wouldn't eat 'em!

Imagine huge things wanting your skin

to make bags out of and to put things in.

Imagine strange beasts wanting your shell

for combs, or jewelry, or a decorative bell.

Imagine being chased from the very beginning!

If you're a Loggerhead turtle there ain't no winning!

What a bummer life is from the very first day

when Mom dumps you on a beach and then swims away.

Instead of being born into soft loving hands

you pop out of an egg and you're buried in sand.

Sand in your eyes, and sand in your nose,

sand in places where the sun never goes.

Heaven forbid that you know where you are

when you make it out of the sand

and you're under the stars

at night

and you have to sprint for your life

to get to the ocean before morning's light.

What if you were born in the ocean

with your arms and legs not built for swimming motion?

That poor little Loggerhead has to sprint through the sand

with tiny flat legs and tiny flat hands.

And aren't you born hungry with maybe a thirst?

Being born a Loggerhead would be kind of a curse!

We humans get wrapped in warm blankets and coddled.

When you're born a Loggerhead

you have to slam down the throttle

to get to your home you're trying to reach -

get in the water and off the beach!

(That's if you were even born at all

and your egg wasn't part of a breakfast call.)

Imagine being born in the middle of a field

and dive bombers and jets want to make you their meal.

By daybreak if you didn't make it to the ocean

above you would begin a grand commotion

when the seagulls would start to swoop and dive!

That's when you have to run for your life!

But hold on! Vultures! Straight up ahead!

Waiting on the ground to snatch you up instead!

Now, yes, it's true, you were born not alone,

you were hatched in a big pile of family your own.

Brothers and sisters having to do the same

as they, too, were born into this not-so-fun game.

I'm sure you've often thought about

your sister being taken

by a big airplane when she awakens.

And I'm sure your brother can be kind of a pain

and you've imagined him being carried off in a train.

But that's what happens on your very first day

when you witness your playmates being hauled away!

Let's just say you make it to the water,

do you think your life is safe and your day is over?

No, because now you're a floating treat

for the frigate birds above you wanting to eat!

Can you remember your first morning

when you were fed warm milk and then took to snoring,

happy and content in your mother's soft arms?

Life for us is a beautiful charm!

Imagine your first morning

being dropped into World War Three?

Wouldn't you think, *Why me?*

Let's just say

on your first day

the escape you made

and you're now in your watery home

where the vastness of the depths is yours to roam.

But don't forget how big you are.

You're about the size of a Hot Wheel car.

Imagine being in a stadium

and you're the only French fry.

Imagine being the only bug in the sky.

Imagine a desert and you're the only ant.

Imagine how small and helpless you'd feel?

I bet you can't.

What a miracle it would be to survive your first day,

the next, and the next, until a year's passed away.

If you're lucky you might make it to the age of three!

Or luckier, still, to twenty-three!

You dodged all the fishing nets swooping around,

the longlines, the gill nets, the trawls on the ground.

You didn't get caught in a trap, dredge, or pot.

Between sharks teeth you were never caught.

You avoided getting choked on a piece of plastic

and swimming through water that was dangerously toxic.

Somehow, some way,

through some grace from the heavens

you made it to the old age of sixty-seven

and grew to your maximum weight.

Wouldn't that be great?

The heaviest Loggerhead ever found

weighed one thousand two hundred and two pounds!

(If you ask me,

that Loggerhead should be wearing a crown!)

Yes, I think those turtles deserve a prize

for just figuring out how to stay alive!

And if I'm lucky enough

to ever see one of those creatures

with its salt-watering eyes and prehistoric features

coming upon the beach to lay its eggs,

I'd let it do its thing and stay far away.

But in my mind I'd shout and say,

'Thank you, Loggerhead, for being here today!'

The Bouncing Billies

It was one of those days

I wasn't needed around the house.

Well, *needed* isn't the right word,

wanted is a better choice.

I had the feeling Mother didn't want me around,

when I asked if I could help

my offers she shot down.

'Can I help sew?'

'No.'

'Can I help mow?'

'No.'

'Can I help make bread?

I'll even mop the floor!

Can I paint the ceiling?

I'm really bored!'

By the answers that I got, the mumbles and grunts,

and the look my mother gave me like I was a runt,

it became clear as day

that in my house that day

it would be the worst kind of way

to spend a summer's day.

So off I went to the attention of no one,

and nobody cared when I left on my own.

Down the stairs I skipped,

over the lawn I tripped,

down the street, and up a block,

down two more, and across a lot.

Through some trees, and over a stream,

passing a wheat field the color of cream.

I found a stick and things to hit

then climbed a rock and had a sit.

The end of my stick I started to rub

on the rock I was sitting on that was hard and rough,

carving a point to make a spear

when something odd

caught my ear.

'We bounce, we bounce, we bounce!

We bounce, we bounce, we bounce!

We bounce, we bounce, we bounce!

We bounce, we bounce, we bounce!'

Now granted I have many thoughts

dancing in my head,

and sometimes it's hard to fall asleep

while I'm thinking in my bed,

but I was very certain

at that moment in time

I was hearing something

outside my frame of mind.

'We bounce, we bounce, we bounce!

We bounce, we bounce, we bounce!'

I stopped making my spear

and sat very still,

and sure enough I heard them

coming over the hill.

I dropped my stick and got to my feet

to get a better view,

when I saw what was making the noise

I wasn't sure if it was true.

I thought maybe I was seeing things

because I had never seen the likes

of what those people were doing

and the manner in which they hiked.

'We bounce, we bounce, we bounce!

We bounce, we bounce, we bounce!

We bounce, we bounce, we bounce!

We bounce, we bounce, we bounce!'

Well there must have been eight or nine of 'em

bouncing through the trees,

and that's when I suddenly realized

they were bouncing straight toward me!

I jumped off the rock and behind it I hid,

with my back to the rock closer I slid.

I sat very still and held my breath,

I guess you could say I was scared to death

as they came bouncing past me from all directions.

I wish I had my spear for at least some protection!

Two bounced past me on my right,

on my left another three,

I counted four more bouncing off the rock

directly over me!

I ducked down and hit the ground,

and me they never saw.

But I heard them very clearly

as they went bouncing along.

'We bounce, we bounce, we bounce!

We bounce, we bounce, we bounce!

We're the Bouncing Billies!

We bounce, we bounce, we bounce!'

They bounced on two feet, this way and that,

and bounced through the trees like a kangaroo pack!

There were no obstacles that caused a delay,

nothing at all got in their way!

Rivers, and rocks, and bushes, and trees

they all bounced past with nimble ease!

When I determined that I was safe

and that they had disappeared,

I began to laugh out loud

at what I once had feared.

A family they were, a bouncing family,

bouncing all together!

A mother, a father, their six kids,

even a bouncing grandmother!

I realized, then, as a got up from the ground

that the bouncing family was headed

straight for town!

Well this was something I couldn't miss

so after them I started to sprint.

I caught up to them as the town's edge they hit,

their bouncing and singing hadn't slowed a bit.

'We bounce, we bounce, we bounce!

We bounce, we bounce, we bounce!

We're the Bouncing Billies!

We bounce, we bounce, we bounce!'

They bounced on cars, and bounced through yards,

and I couldn't believe my eyes

when they bounced straight into my town

as a bird would fly.

I had a hard time keeping up with their bouncing

as they bounced, and bounced, and bounced.

So I decided I would do the same,

and I bounced, and I bounced, and I bounced.

I followed them bouncing through a backdoor

and we bounced and we bounced

through a grocery store.

Over the meats and a vegetable stand,

when we passed the chips

I grabbed a few in my hand.

We bounced into a hotel

and bounced on all the beds.

Instead of going around the theatre

we bounced right through it instead!

We bounced down every aisle,

and we bounced on every seat,

and as we bounced through the exit

our song we did repeat.

'We're the Bouncing Billies!

We bounce, we bounce, we bounce!

We're the Bouncing Billies!

We bounce, we bounce, we bounce!'

Through a museum with fine art on the wall

we bounced very carefully so no piece would fall.

When we bounced through the library it was a riot,

over chairs and desks we disturbed the quiet.

'We're the Bouncing Billies!

We bounce, we bounce, we bounce!

We're the Bouncing Billies!

We bounce, we bounce, we bounce!'

But while I was bouncing and singing my song

I heard a voice that was louder and much more strong.

'Billie!' I heard.

'BILLIEEE!'

I turned with a bounce to see my mom

who at the time wasn't singing along.

'Hello, Mom!' I sang,

because I was sure she wasn't knowing

who I was and what I was doing.

'I'm the Bouncing Billie!

I bounce, I bounce, I bounce!

I'm the Bouncing Billie!

I bounce around the house!'

With her hands on her hips she tightened her lips

with a scowl that made me shiver.

It was clear right then

my game she would end

with the words she was about to deliver.

'We're the bouncing Billies—!' I started,

hoping she might change her mind

and join me in my bouncing game

so we could sing in time.

'We're the Bouncing Bill—'

'Billie! That's enough!' she shouted

cutting my singing short.

With a clap, and a snap, and a finger to the ground

she immediately changed my course.

'Get off of the couch right now, young lady,

and stop bouncing around the house!

Go to your room immediately

and not another word out of your mouth!'

Without saying more

she grabbed the lamp from the floor

and put it on its stand,

and showed me my direction

with an outstretched hand.

Now at obeying my mother I'm not the best,

and I know that if I weren't around

she'd probably get more rest.

And by the look she was giving me

and her upset demeanor

that suggested I was currently

pinning the trouble meter

I thought it best to go to my room

just as she had said.

So that's where I am with a voice that's low

bouncing quietly on my bed.

'I'm the Bouncing Billie,' I whisper,

'I bounce, I bounce, I bounce.

But never upon the furniture

of my mother's house.'

The Greatest Baseball Team Ever

I'm not the tallest

of the bunch.

There's Jared's limp

and Arnie's hunch.

Billy has big buckteeth,

Roland's skin gives me the creeps.

Harvey's shaped like a bowling ball,

Lenny's boney and awkwardly tall.

Farris is the poorest one -

if clothes need two to match

he'll be wearing only one.

Yet he's not the saddest case

although his life is tough,

Tony only has one eye,

and on a baseball field that's rough.

We were all born in Kokomodiddle,

a town that's big but we think it's little,

at the same time, in the same place.

People claim we came from space.

I can't blame them and perhaps they're correct

how nine different kids came to connect;

how nine different kids from nine different moms,

from nine different dads, living on nine different farms,

how we all at once, in one big bunch,

came into this world…

It's crazy stuff.

We were all born on the same night

in an electrical storm that took out the lights.

The thunder crashed and the rain splashed down.

It was the worst storm ever in our town.

But when it was over, when it was done,

there were nine more babies under the sun.

I'm certain

it was determined

on that very night

we'd be friends for life.

And, yes, it's true, friends we would be.

But that's only part of the story, you see.

We didn't all meet right away,

seven years had passed to the day.

And on that day to a lot we would stray

at the beginning of summer at the end of May.

It was a vacant lot of dirt and stone,

broken bottles, weeds, and an old cow bone.

Hot and dusty

not a bit of shade did it yield.

But that barren place would become

our baseball field.

Somehow, someway, we all had the itch

to leave our homes and the families we'd ditch.

We all had gloves and baseball hats,

some brought balls, some brought bats.

We were seven years old on the dot

when we met on that desolate plot.

I'll never forget the looks on our faces

as we stood in a circle in silent gazes.

It took some time to take it all in,

but soon we were breaking out in grins.

It was as if we were part of some funny joke

as we stared at each other while no one spoke.

But we all knew we were there for a reason

and that was to begin baseball season.

It was Harvey who was the first to speak.

'I want to be pitcher,' he said with a squeak.

A pitcher? we all thought at the same time.

Fat little Harvey? A pitcher? What a crime!

'If that's the case, then I'm the catcher!'

said Lenny, hitting his round mitt of leather.

Now those of us who were in the know

of how to play the game

looked at each other with furrowed brows,

looks of grief,

faces of shame.

It really wasn't starting off great,

our team was doomed right out of the gate.

The shortest and fattest to be our *pitcher*?

The tallest and skinniest to be our *catcher*?

And as if it couldn't get worse

Tony shouted with a burst,

'I'm playing first!'

Oh my! The kid with one eye!

I thought with a sigh as I looked up to the sky.

What next? Oh let me guess,

the kid with the limp,

the kid with the gimp,

is going to pick the largest turf.

'Center field!' Jared shouted. Of course!

Here's the thing, in the outfield

you have to look up to the sky,

when hunched-over Arnie took left field

I thought we'd all die.

The kid with the bad face went out to right,

the bucktoothed kid took second,

which left me and poor Farris…

And it turned out how I reckoned.

When Farris picked shortstop my heart nearly stopped -

and not because he was wearing cowboy boots

handed down from his pops -

what scared me the most, and what made my legs shake,

was the position *I* was forced to take.

Third base?

Are you kidding?

For me that position was strictly forbidden!

The hardest hit balls over rocks and debris

coming a million miles an hour straight toward me!

Ground balls and line drives bouncing and buzzing,

they don't call it The Hot Corner for nothing!

That day was quite a spectacle as you can imagine,

a circus, a charade, a comedy pageant.

Dropped balls, foul balls, lost balls in the weeds;

missed pitches, missed bases made us angry indeed.

It didn't help that the day was horribly hot,

and the dust that we raised made all of us cough.

If we played in the middle of a desert

it couldn't have been hotter.

(Of course no one thought about bringing water.)

Shouting and cursing the more frustrated we got…

The game ended with a brawl on that lot.

All of us taking to pushing and shoving,

calling each other names not very becoming.

I took a fist on the nose, and a boot on the rump,

and came home crying with bruises and lumps.

I wasn't the only one,

we were all sad and beaten.

That was the first and last day of that baseball season.

We didn't see each other for an entire year

and if we passed each other on the street

we'd give just a sneer.

But I knew what was happening,

I had a feeling of sorts,

we were all doing our own thing,

taking our course,

to practice and play every day of the week,

alone, by ourselves, with no one to speak.

I rigged an old lawnmower to launch ground balls,

and hit my own pitches into an empty horse stall.

As I did this I wondered about the others,

and if, in some way, our team might recover.

But little did I realize, little did I know,

how the others practiced on their own.

Harvey with his stubby body

was spending his days making a hobby

of learning how to throw every type of pitch.

When he was done, his arms he'd switch.

Lenny was doing squats in his barn.

Roland was working on his arm

by throwing potatoes as far as he could.

His old ax handle was a splintered piece of wood

he used as a bat.

If you think it's hard to hit a curveball

try hitting one with that.

Arnie watched bird shadows when he had lunch

because with his hunch

looking down

was much easier than looking up.

Watching those shadows the better he'd know

exactly where a fly ball might go.

A shortstop has to be fast and quick

and my dad's old cowboy boots I wouldn't have picked

to be my first footwear for agility and speed,

but poor Farris was always in need.

That year he spent catching mice in his house.

Even with fast shoes it's hard to catch a mouse.

One-eyed Tony was wearing a blindfold,

I was later told,

in an empty root cellar that was rather cold.

He'd throw a rubber ball as hard as he could

and the rubber ball did what a rubber ball should

bouncing this way and that off of crack and stone.

He'd use his ears and in on it he'd hone

until he knew where it was so he could reach out and grab it.

With one swift motion, he'd snag it.

Billy would have been better off getting braces,

instead he was having personal races

challenging every kid he met

to a sixty-foot footrace bet.

It just so happened all those that he beckoned

would help him go faster from first to second.

Which left our center fielder, the one with the hobble,

when he ran with his limp

he looked like he wobbled.

It was hard to watch that only day of our first season.

Why he wanted to play baseball was beyond our reason.

But Mom always says, 'Everything runs its course.'

I heard he practiced his baseball while riding a horse.

That notion would leave me scratching my head,

so I let it 'run its course' instead.

A year had passed and we all turned eight,

and I, myself, just couldn't wait

to get on that field and get back on that lot

so we could give the game just one more shot.

We all came together

pounding our leather

with scowls, and grunts, and exaggerated frowns.

We looked each other up and down,

some of us even spat on the ground

while a hot breeze blew dust around.

With feelings spilling over from last year

we didn't say a word as we took to the field.

We played four-on-four with a permanent pitcher,

playing our positions and taking turns being hitter.

If there was improvement we couldn't see it

which made us madder than last year, and I mean it.

I spent all day yelling, 'Give me a hit!'

as I pounded the dust out of my mitt.

I never got to show the others

that I could swipe up a ground ball like no other.

I wanted to show everyone how I practiced

day in and day out.

I got so angry, 'Hit the ball!' I did shout.

That entire day I didn't get one hit,

so frustrated I yelled, 'I quit!'

'Me too!' someone followed.

'You all stink!' someone hollered.

But instead of leaving and going our own way

we all came together with something to say

with more bad words we had learned over the year.

(If a preacher were present it would have burned his ears.)

And, yes, we were older and one year bigger...

How that day ended you could probably figure.

Punches, bruises, scars, and scrapes;

bleeding noses, and scratches,

no one escaped.

So that was it! I was done!

From the idea of baseball I would personally run!

After that day I hated the game!

The word *baseball* - I didn't even want to hear the name!

Here's the thing, I always loved the game.

I have a poster of the Little League World Series

hanging in a frame.

(That I took off the wall and kicked under my bed

after coming home with an aching head.)

I'd look at that poster all the time,

and to that stadium I'd go in my mind

thinking about how great it would be

to lead a team to victory.

To be part of a team year after year;

a team that got better until the fans all cheered,

'That's the greatest Little League team we've ever seen!'

Yes, into that poster I always dreamed…

Four years passed, again to the day,

the thought of baseball far away,

when I saw a flyer on a telephone pole

of a circus in town and I thought I'd go.

It just so happened that the circus tent

sat exactly where my time was spent

thinking I would be part of a team…

The place where I had

lost a dream.

Our entire infield that circus tent covered,

and seeing it there made me shudder.

I got a queasiness in my stomach

and was about to turn around,

then I swallowed dryly

and into my hand I looked down

at the ticket I held that cost me a bundle.

'A month's worth of work,' I mumbled.

So into the tent I stumbled and wandered.

Why is it so dark in here? I wondered.

But I found a seat, and in it I sat,

and waited in the darkness while my feet I tapped.

And then suddenly, with a boom and a crash,

all the lights blasted on with a flash!

From a great smoke cloud a man appeared

wearing a red cape, with a long white beard;

he had a glittery top hat, and a suit that sparkled.

Just looking at him was quite a marvel!

He spun in a circle and said in a deep voice,

'Welcome! Welcome! And remember your choice

to be part of this adventure, part of this show!

When I leave

it's *magic* you will know!'

Well, I thought, that sounded grand to me -

if I can't play baseball maybe a magician I'll be.

I looked hard in the dark to see if I could see any others,

but I couldn't, and began to wonder

if I was the only one there, the only one at the show.

A chill went up my spine and I thought I might go.

But another flash!

I heard something explode!

When the smoke cleared

the man was on the highest tent pole!

How he got up there I hadn't a clue,

but then he let go, and around the tent he flew!

I looked as hard as I could for a rope or a wire

and how he created his act as a flier.

But I saw nothing, nothing at all;

when he landed in the lights

I sat there in awe.

And then again a big, *Vavoom!*,

another sparkling flash filled the room!

The next thing that happened was the oddest of all,

I never felt myself move, I never felt myself fall;

I never felt myself move out of my seat,

so I don't know how I ended up on my feet.

All of us were there, standing in a circle,

around the large old man that glittered and sparkled.

With darkness all around us

upon us bright lights shined.

There we all were,

all of us nine.

We all had wide eyes and looks of doubt

how any of this could come about.

'You!' the sparkling old man pointed his wand at me.

'What position do you play?'

'Huh?' I croaked, too scared to say.

'What? Don't you know English? Or can't you hear?

How about you?' he turned, to Lenny's look of fear.

'C-c-catcher,' Lenny said,

his voice quivering and shaking.

'C-c-catcher?' the old man repeated, as if imitating.

'And you!' the man spun, pointing his wand again,

and when he did beams of sparks it sent!

Toward Arnie this time, 'Left field you play?'

But the man boomed before Arnie could say.

'Left field? *Left field?* You have to be kidding!

This idea of baseball from your minds you need ridding!'

He spun around and from his wand fire flew!

'You, and you, and you, and you!

You know nothing about baseball and I'll tell you why!'

By then I was so scared I had tears in my eyes.

'You're misfits, and cripples,

and I'm sure when you eat

you spill your food around your feet!

You're delinquents and ne'er-do-wells!'

(I saw that my eyes weren't the only ones

starting to well.

I could see what was happening

was scaring the others.)

'You think you're baseball players? Why bother?

You know it's something to be good at your position

but if you want to be ballplayers to me you should listen!'

He whipped his wand through the air

to an enormous crash!

The tent went up in flames and turned into cloudy ash!

Suddenly the others were sitting in a dugout

in the middle of a stadium with an umpire yelling, 'You're out!'

At me he was shouting while I held my bat

wondering seriously where I was 'at'.

Now I know that's not swell English but at that moment

I didn't care,

for all around me, and down at me,

an entire *stadium* did stare.

The umpire pointed to the dugout to where I should go,

and to there I walked, dumfounded and slow,

as I gazed around me looking about.

I was in the same stadium, there was no doubt.

The same stadium that hung on my wall

where they had the Little League World Series

at the beginning of fall.

The scoreboard, the boxes, the Megavision screen…

I was in the same stadium, the stadium of my dreams!

And there in the dugout, there they all were

with looks like mine that asked, *'What just occurred?'*

'Come on boys! Wake up!'

an older man clapped,

wearing the same uniform and cap.

He had the same long beard,

he was the same old man

who was just in the tent with a wand in his hand.

There we all sat wearing uniforms that read

Kokomodiddle in fine cursive thread.

As we all looked around, dazed and confused,

the man shouted at us again, 'You're gonna lose!'

He pointed to the scoreboard and the numbers it read.

'Thirteen to nothing!' he said.

'You boys better start playing like a team,

a team, a team, A T-E-A *EEEAM!'*

Smash! Bam! Another explosion!

A wave-crashing sound like a tsunami from the ocean!

A crack of lightning!

A blinding light!

It all happened in the blink of an eye!

Before we knew what hit us,

before we knew what to do,

we found ourselves in the dirt

when we all came to.

We sat up, blinking, at the same time

as if we had just woken up, all of us nine,

wondering how we ended up on the ground

as we slowly sat up around our pitching mound.

We were back on our field, the tent was gone,

so, too, was the sparkling old man

with his fire-shooting wand.

We got to our feet and dusted ourselves

knowing full well

that very same day

we were all turning twelve.

We all knew that our birthdays had come,

and we knew after this year Little League was done.

And, somehow, silently, we all knew what to do

because of that strange moment

we had just been through.

We picked up our mitts and bats,

adjusted our caps,

and quietly took to the field

with an excitement and energy we could all feel.

It would take hours to replay all of our games,

but let me tell you it was pretty insane

how we handled every opponent,

took on every team,

until I found myself

living my dream.

It was the Little League World Series

and there we all were

sitting in the dugout

after a playoff world tour.

But things didn't look so great,

we were down by thirteen,

just as it was in our circus tent dream.

The old man wasn't there

it was just us nine

looking at each other

because we knew it was time.

It was the top of the eighth

and the fans were starting to leave.

To think we could win this game

one would have to believe

we'd be sent home hanging our heads

unless we had

something up our sleeve.

As we sat there in the dugout

we heard the umpire shout,

'Come on boys!

You're delaying the game!

Back on the field!'

But we felt no shame.

'They should quit!' someone shouted from the stands.

'Go home!' another yelled through their hands.

'Kokomodiddle is a joke!'

'They can't play ball!'

'How did they even make it to the Series at all?'

Surrounded by the booing crowd,

getting more angry,

getting more loud,

we looked at each other and started to smile,

even though we were down by a mile.

Our smiles then turned into giggling laughs

because we all knew we were going to come back.

We planned it out from the very beginning.

We planned it out from the very first inning.

We all knew how the game would go

because we were putting on

a magic show.

We scripted it out all year long

as we beat team after team

and strengthened our bond.

We'd go into the Championship looking silly and slow

as if the game we didn't know.

And we all played our part to a tee

which is why we looked at each other with such glee.

We were all smiling

because it was going as planned,

and our smiles got bigger as we listened to the fans.

The other team, they had never seen us before.

They didn't know the burden we bore.

When everyone first saw us take the field

we knew the reaction it would yield.

When Farris ran out in his cowboy boots

the other team started to laugh and hoot.

When hunched-over Arnie took left field

gasps from the audience we could all hear.

When Billy smiled and showed his teeth

half the audience let out a screech.

Harvey threw pitches and purposely missed,

that's when the fans started to hiss.

Tony pretended he was scared of the ball

acting like he couldn't see it at all.

The funniest was the hit to Roland

when everybody at him was hollerin',

'Fly ball!' 'Fly ball!' 'Roland, fly ball!'

But he pretended not to notice at all.

Instead he decided to pick at his face

and look at fingers in disgrace.

We all did our best to stifle our laughs

as the baseball over his head did pass.

Yes, this was why we delayed the game

because we were laughing at the way we played.

But now it was time for the real game to start

and show the fans a team with heart.

For we were the boys from Kokomodiddle

who had known each other since we were little.

We came together with our hands in the middle,

looked into each other's eyes,

and shouted,

'Kokomodiddle!'

We took the field with pride and glory…

You can probably guess the end of this story.

The first thing that happened

was Harvey taking the mound.

(Our hearts alit to the booing crowd!)

He had pitched the entire game with his right arm,

now with his left he was about to charm.

For he threw better with his left than the latter.

That's why I kept shouting,

'Hey batter, batter! Hey batter, batter!'

I snapped up a grounder and threw it to first.

Farris pulled a double-play in a cowboy-boot burst.

It was an easy three outs

and when we got to the plate

the fans were in a shocked sort of state

when we whopped four homers

and brought three others in.

Billy stole all his bases with a bucktoothed grin.

The top of the ninth ended with three more quick outs,

the last fly ball leaving no doubt

that our team was much better than we pretended to be

when Jared ran down a fly ball

impossibly.

It was a line-drive headed over the fence

but limping Jared never gave it a chance.

When he ran, and jumped, and caught it in the air

even all of us did stare.

He galloped, yes *galloped*, as fast as a horse!

Mother was right, everything runs its course.

The game ended when I hit a grand slam.

I'd brag about it, but that's not the person I am.

I'm the person who likes to stare at the wall

at my Little League World Series poster

and those kids playing ball.

I can swear that the photo comes alive

and the tiny players and the fans turn into real life.

I can see my tiny self playing with all my tiny friends,

and I'll watch the game from beginning to end.

There have been some great teams

like the Sox and the Yanks.

There have been some great players

like Babe, Lou, and Hank.

And Little League baseball might not be the greatest

because it's only kids under the pre-teen ages.

And our Kokomodiddle win has since been forgotten

by family and friends and those who were watching.

But I know there are nine of us out there,

nine of us who cared,

nine of us who loved baseball,

nine of us who dared

to overcome our hindrances and physical ills,

end our differences, and work on our skills.

And I'll never forget the magic man in the tent

and the magical message to us he sent,

that in order to fulfill our baseball dreams

we better come together and play like a team.

And I'll never forget that magical day

when we won the World Series in our magical way.

And I'll never forget, I'll always remember…

I played on

the greatest baseball team ever.

The Ugly Worm

There was an ugly worm

who had a bit of strife.

She just happened to be

the ugliest worm in life.

During a time in an ancient place

long before the human race

when there were only plants and worms,

worms, and worms, and worms, and worms.

In an era of muck and mire,

swamps, and pits, and volcano fire,

mud bogs, and stinky goop,

when all the worms swam in primordial soup.

To be the ugliest worm

was really quite a feat,

for there existed many worms,

most of them not so neat.

Some worms had thousands of eyes,

others thousands of toes,

some had prickly hairs

growing on their prickly nose.

Some had warts,

others dots,

some smelled of stinky feet,

some bubbled and gurgled

and looked like goobers

in the humid heat.

Some spewed slime when they slithered,

others a noxious gas.

It wasn't a land of pretty worms

but our worm came in last.

'Look at that thing!' the worms would shout

as the ugly worm wiggled about.

'What is it?'

'What could it be?'

'That's the ugliest worm I've ever seen!'

'Is it really one of us?'

'What exactly is it?'

'Did it come from another planet?'

'Is it here just to visit?'

But the little worm had feelings of care,

she never liked it when the other worms stared.

She didn't like to be the butt of a joke

and hear all the mean things

the other worms spoke.

So everyday she would wander off

to where the other worms were not.

She'd find caves for swimming, and holes for hiding,

slippery rocks just right for sliding.

She'd squeeze herself through cracks and crags

and roll around in musty slag.

She'd ball up in the muck,

and stretch out in the mire,

and at the end of her playful day,

to her home she would retire.

But the ugly worm's adventures

weren't helping with her looks

and all the worms took notice

of the toll it took.

For when she returned she was more ugly than before,

something impossible the other worms swore.

She'd return from her trips with scars, and contusions,

scrapes, and burns, and swollen protrusions.

Upon her return the worms would shout,

'Can she get any uglier?'

'That we doubt!'

Well it just so happened

after one fun day

of playing in a place

far away

the ugly worm returned to a bit of a ruckus,

all the worms had gathered and on her they were focused.

'You're too ugly!'

'Too ugly to stay!'

'That's right, ugly worm, you must leave right away!'

'You're scaring the kids!'

'You're ugly as sin!'

'You're even uglier than the ugly worm

you had once been!'

'It's safe to say you're now no longer a worm!'

'You're something that looks like it came out of a storm!'

'Your looks are disgraceful!'

'We don't want you around!'

'Your looks are quite frankly bringing us down!'

So they kicked her out,

they shooed her away,

and the ugly worm

had no place to stay.

She inched alone, crying and sad.

Her life had become lonelier than the lonely life

she once had.

'What's the point of living?' to herself she would ask.

'This hard life has become too great of a task.

I've been so ugly, so ugly from the start

and it's hard to inch along

with such a heavy heart.

No one knows what it feels like

to never have a friend,

I'm thinking it might be best

to bring my ugly life to an end.'

Aimlessly she crawled, day after day,

inching along to nowhere, with no place to stay.

Day after day, so sad and so slow,

wriggling by herself with no place to go.

With tears in her eyes and a broken heart

she came to a place where the earth did part.

It was a tree in the mud

that shot up to the sky.

'That I will climb,' the ugly warm said,

'and jump off and die.'

High up in the tree

the worm did climb

to end her life, to end her time

from a place not nice from the start.

She'd hang from a branch, and let go,

and from her sad life she'd depart.

So high, so high, so very high up in the tree

she hung upside down and counted to three.

'One!' she counted, for on three she'd let go.

'Two!' she counted, and on

'Three!' she let go!

But something happened…

Something strange…

When she reached three,

three never came.

What happened instead was a deep state of slumber

as she hung from her toes from a tiny bit of lumber.

Hanging so high, so high in the sky,

she never would fall, she never would die.

She was possessed by a sleep

that lasted for weeks.

And the dreams - *Wow!* - they were like no other!

She dreamt she was wrapped in a warm caring cover;

a cover so loving of warmth and hotness

that touched her and massaged her

in caressing softness.

And inside of this cover, this cocoon if you will,

her body was changing into something unreal -

into something with colors so clear and so bright;

into something with wings that could take off in flight!

What happened next within this strange dream

was a door opened up, or so it seemed.

Her cocoon split open out she fell!

'Aaah!' she screamed! 'Aaah!' she yelled!

Spiraling down, the world rushed by!

'Help!' she shouted! 'Help!' she cried!

She closed her eyes and said, 'This is it!

I'm going to die when the ground I hit!'

But gradually her falling slowed,

and she felt her body expand and grow!

She had wings! Beautiful wings!

The wings she saw in her dream

with radiant colors never before seen

of yellows, and blues, reds, and greens

reflecting the light in a glorious sheen!

Spreading them wide she felt the breeze

lifting her up

to glide

with ease!

'I'm flying! I'm flying! I can fly through the sky!

Weee!' she shouted. *'Weee!'* she cried!

She spun, and she twirled, and in circles she flew

as the first flying creature the world ever knew!

'Yippee!' she wailed

as she sailed,

seeing from up high

everything from the sky.

And as she looked down

at everything on the ground

she got a better view

of the world she once knew.

She saw how the world was so vast and so grand

and wondered how she could ever think

about leaving her land.

Soon she was flying over her home

and over the worms she had once known.

They all came out to look up at the sky

for never in their lives had they seen something fly.

And not only could it fly but it was beautiful too!

Such lovely colors the world never knew!

'Aaah!' said some worms,

and others said, *'Oooh!'*

as over them she flew.

And as she did she shouted down,

'I love you! I love you all!' to her old worm town.

Then off she flew into a sun setting low

to the *oohs* and the *aahs* of the worms below.

By the sound of the voice all the worms knew

it was the ugliest worm that over them flew.

Flying off she would never know

how she affected all the worms below.

Worm town was quiet for a very long time

while all the worms thought about what they saw in the sky.

It made them think and change their thoughts.

A great lesson the worms were taught.

For the most beautiful thing they had ever seen

was once the ugliest worm that had ever been.

After that the worms smiled and gave a heartfelt, *'Hi!'*,

to all the ugly worms when they passed by.

They never forgot what they saw in the sky -

that beautiful thing

called the butterfly.

They never forgot as they wriggled and slithered

that the ugliest worm

just might be

the next

caterpillar.

Counting My Blessings

I didn't know what blessings were

but I was told to count 'em.

But how was I supposed to count 'em

when they didn't even exist?

Well they must exist I told myself

or I wouldn't have been told to count 'em.

So I thought, and I wondered,

I grieved, and I pondered:

a blessing, a blessing, *a blessing*?

Is it round, is it square, short, or tall?

Is it something that lives in a tree?

Can it bounce, or roll,

walk, or talk?

Is it something I can get for free?

Maybe it smells, or it's just a thing,

like a ball, or a toy, or a bouncy spring.

Can it jump, or skip,

or fly like a bird?

A *blessing* is such a confusing word.

Perhaps it's something I can't even see,

like my breath, or a ghost, or a tiny flea.

Or it lives in water, or underground.

Maybe it's always behind me.

Do they run in packs? Are they solitary creatures?

Do they even socialize at all?

With honks, or squeaks, or computer tweets,

or a bellowing, echoing call?

These blessings I tell you

they got on my nerves.

I couldn't sleep, I tossed and turned.

I rolled around on top of my bed,

tried every position, and stood on my head.

I slept not a wink

as my mind did think

what a blessing could possibly be,

and spent the day

tired and cranky

looking for a blessing to see.

I looked behind my sister,

and under the car,

stood on my tiptoes to look real far.

My parents' closet had nothing to offer,

the dusty attic was quite a cougher.

Dad yelled at me to get off of the roof.

My older brother called me a goof

when he found me in the bathtub

face to the drain.

I thought I'd see one in the pipes

if my eyes I did strain.

Into the bushes, did it live with the snipes?

Mother was concerned about all the hype.

'What's all this activity, this running about?

And why do you look like you're about to pout?'

And just as she said that

that's what I did.

I flopped down at the table,

hands to my head,

spilled my thoughts,

sobbed and said,

'Not even one! I couldn't even count *one*!'

'One wha—?' my mom started.

'Blessing!' I shouted before she was done.

'Blessing?' she asked, confused and calm.

'Yes!' I yelled back, wiping my tears with a palm.

And then there was silence, still and quiet,

as my mother listened to my sniffling riot.

She sat there patiently, her head at a tilt,

thinking about the words I had spilt.

'Hmm,' she said. 'I think someone needs a nap—'

'No!' I screamed, with a terrible snap.

But it didn't take long before I was stumbling to bed

to my soft space to rest my head.

When I awoke my mind was in a fog,

I didn't know if I was a human, a bird, a dog, or a frog.

But I thought about something that had come in my dream -

a feeling, a vision, or so it did seem.

I remembered everything that day

that came and went or got in my way.

In my dream

I was told

everything had meaning.

Whether new, or old,

or dirty and needing a cleaning;

big, or small,

smelly, or tasty;

my brother, my sister, my morning pastry;

my father, my mother, the roof over my head;

the food in the cupboard,

the tools in the shed.

My dream! It showed me!

I was no longer guessing

what that thing was

that was called a blessing!

Suddenly I was feeling happy and refreshed!

I bet you can imagine what I did if you guessed!

I sat up in bed, and that's right, started counting!

The sun – that's one! The air – that's two!

I counted and counted until my face turned blue!

Now I can tell you, I know for certain,

I ended my counting with the living room curtains.

I found them spectacular in a new kind of way

although they're stained and an off shade of gray.

I could wrap myself in them and hide from the others.

If worse came to worse I could use them as covers.

I could shake them back and forth

and pretend I'm the wind,

or wrap them over my head like a long-haired wig.

One hundred and eighty-two

blessings I counted when I was through!

That's when I let out a victorious sigh -

I didn't even know I could count that high!

And wasn't that a blessing? That I could even count?

Counting my blessings wore me out.

But what I had learned while chasing a blessing

was nothing but a great big lesson!

Now I don't count

but in my head I do shout,

A blessing! A blessing! A blessing!

Because Of The Tree

I saw some bikes

all familiar to me

scattered under a tall pine tree.

All my friends' bikes were parked

under the tallest tree in our local park.

I was pedaling home

(from where I don't know)

and when I saw the bikes

I rode real slow.

I drifted toward them until I saw

all of the bikes, and I knew them all.

And I knew that tree, and I knew my friends,

and I knew that they were climbing it again.

I looked at the sky and then up in the tree.

They must be at the top, none of them could I see.

But there was an issue,

it was getting dark,

and it wasn't a good time

to start playing in the park.

Before dark was when I had to be home.

I looked at the sky and its glowing dome.

Yes, the sun had set

but there was still twilight yet.

I could climb that tree and get home I bet

before it was dark,

before it was night.

The sky still had a *little* light.

So I jumped off my bike and started to climb

as fast as I could to make some time

to get to the top and say hello to my friends,

before I had to come back down again.

I had climbed the tree so many times before

and I knew each branch and the handhold it bore.

At least at the bottom where the branches were fat

and soft with the climbing of many hands past.

And they were spread out enough

to have no fear

of hitting my head

or scraping my ears.

So I followed the worn path

of previous climbers

making good time through the forgiving timbers,

until I got to the tree's middle

where the path started to get little.

I had to slow down and pick my way,

the smooth path below

had gone away.

But I couldn't quit, I was past the halfway mark,

and even though it was getting dark

I had to surprise my friends

and make it to the top.

I couldn't just *stop*!

I picked, and weaved,

and rushed through the ascent.

If I wasn't in a hurry

I'm sure I would have spent

more time deciphering the route above me.

Instead I plowed forth, you could say, haphazardly.

Branches poked me in the back

and scraped my arms and face;

I slipped and banged my knee

but I kept my climbing pace.

Even though a sharp branch caught my shirt

and I heard a little tear,

and there were twigs and needles in my hair,

and the rough bark

made marks

upon my legs,

and my arm muscles began to ache,

I still climbed up, I still climbed on

knowing daytime was almost gone.

Now when you get close to the top

during this time in the summer

it isn't the easiest, in fact it's a bummer

because all of the branches have sprouted new twigs

with hard new needles and rough-barked sprigs.

When grabbing a branch you need to be wise,

you might even want to squint your eyes.

The branches at the top can grow so close together -

I always wished at this point I was covered in leather.

The piney branches are so thick at the top of the tree

even during midday you can't really see.

But this time it was darker,

I might say pitch black.

When I cried, '*Hey, guys?*'

no one called back.

'*Are you up there?*'

Again no response.

So I gave one last push

to get to the top.

At last I broke through

and it became oh so true

that I was alone at the top of the tree!

No one was there!

Just me!

We always climb this tree

because it's the tallest,

and when you get to the top

there's a seat for all of us.

In this special tree the very top is flat.

And in many times past

we'd look at the city around us

and start to discuss

how high we were.

That's when we would all refer

to the apartment building next to the park.

(That was lit up with lights now that it was dark!)

We're as high as the fifth story, some would say.

More like the top of the fourth, others claimed.

But at the moment it mattered not

just how far in the air I got,

because as it stood

I was all alone,

at the top of a tree,

far from my home.

And maybe because I was at the top of the tree

a tiny bit of glowing sky I could see,

far in the horizon,

the last bit of light.

But everywhere else

looked like night.

In my mind I said, *It isn't dark yet*,

even though, long ago, the sun had set.

That's when I heard a shout from below,

'Corey, are you up there?' they all wanted to know.

'Yes!' I shouted down as loud as I could.

'Why?' they shouted up as if I should

have known that it was too late to climb.

'We all have to go home! It's dinner time!'

'I climbed up here because I thought you guys were up here!'

'But we weren't! We were at the playground

over there!'

'Oh!'

I shouted below.

'We have to be home

before dark!

And it's already dark!

We have to go!'

'Okay!' I shouted down.

And then mumbled to myself,

'I know.'

I heard them gathering their bikes and telling their jokes,

and I watched them ride off with their colored light spokes -

all on the ground,

all heading home,

while I was five stories high,

in a tree,

all alone.

Below me I could see the first few branches

that drifted down into a well of darkness.

All I really wanted to do was have a good cry.

That's when I looked up at the clear, cloudless sky

and saw all the twinkling stars above me,

so many stars it made me dizzy.

But I knew I had to drop as fast as I could

because I'm sure, by now, as Mother would

be on her phone to all her friends

and was on the very verge to send

police cars and firetrucks to look for me.

I had no choice, I had to get out of the tree.

It was kind of like a slow motion fall,

and if you asked me later I couldn't recall

how I slid down getting bruised and scraped

as the bark of the tree my body it slaked.

I hopped on my bike and rode hard and fast

with the street lamps above me flashing past.

I tossed my bike in the shed,

brushed debris from my head,

and into the kitchen I crept.

Mom was on the phone,

my brother and sister were sitting alone,

and into my seat I leapt.

And just as I whispered not to say a word

my little brother shouted out with a burst,

'Corey's here!'

Now I wouldn't say Mom was shedding tears

but I could tell she was very near.

The worry on her face

then turned to anger.

'I was worried about you! You're late!

I thought you were in danger!'

'No, I—' I started to mumble.

My sister said, 'You're in trouble!'

'Hush, Cynthia!' my mother snapped,

and then stared at me like a steel bear trap.

'What's your excuse this time and it better be good?

And why are you so dirty and covered in wood?

And what's in your hair?

And there's blood on your cheek!'

Mother's voice wasn't calm, it was more like a shriek.

'I— I—' I began again, but didn't know what to say.

How was I going to explain the end of my day

and why I was alone,

on my own,

just me

at the top of a tree

in the park,

in the dark?

'I'm waiting,' she said.

My brother repeated,

'She's waiting,' he said.

My mother didn't stay seated,

she got up from her seat with an up-swung hand.

'That's enough out of you, Stanley, you understand?'

As my sister and brother slumped in their chairs

Mother gave me another demanding stare.

'Well?' she inquired, her temper not receding

while I pretended everything was fine

and began my eating.

'Not another bite until you tell me where you were!'

By the tone of her voice I knew I had better concur.

I cleared my throat, and set down my fork,

and searched my brain for an excuse to report.

I could blame it on my friends

who parked their bikes under the tree.

They did it on purpose! Just to confuse me!

Well that excuse wouldn't work, I was certain,

because with that excuse came the burden

of having to explain why I was alone at the top of a tree

while none of my friends were with me.

I couldn't blame my friends so that excuse I did end.

While I was thinking, Mother asked, *'Well?'* again.

So if I couldn't blame my friends

maybe their bikes I could blame,

because if I didn't see the bikes

my path I wouldn't have changed.

But then I'd have to tell the rest of the story

about how I ended up alone, in the dark,

higher than four stories.

'Still waiting,' Mother said, her anger not abating.

'If you want to go to bed without dinner

you keep delaying!'

Well I was as hungry as ever while before me steamed

one of my favorites - a bowl of mac and cheese.

I was tired of thinking

so I just went with my next thought.

'It was the tree…

Yeah!

It was the tree's fault!'

Now I'm lying in my bed

with sap on my head,

sent to my room without dinner.

(I guess that excuse wasn't the winner.)

The stifled laughing of my brother and sister

chimes in my head as I feel my blisters.

But it was the tree's fault!

It truly was!

But I never got to expound on the cause.

Because it's tall!

Because it's there!

And on its crown, natural chairs!

And when you get to the top you're in the greatest spot

to see everything you know,

and you turn real big

with a miniature world below!

It's like being an eagle in its nest

after soaring through the sky!

Or a king upon his throne

ruling over all mankind!

And even though my stomach's gurgling

and my body's full of aches,

there's an energy running through me,

something I just can't shake.

I was by myself, all alone, high above the ground,

in my favorite tree

during a quiet night

over the muffled city's sound.

Below me on the gridded streets

I saw the lights of tiny toy cars.

And above me,

something I had never seen -

a sky full of shimmering stars.

Digging To China

A swell idea came to me one day

while I was standing in my sandbox.

So I got down on my hands and knees

and decided to follow my thoughts.

A castle I would build,

one that I could live in,

I'd make the walls out of sand and mud,

it would even have a kitchen.

With cupped hands I began to dig,

and dig, and dig, and dig.

And then I wondered how far I could

dig, and dig, and dig.

I thought it would be really grand

to dig all the way to another land.

I imagined myself digging through the Earth

and popping out of the dirt

head first

to the surprised look of a Mongolian child

playing next to his yurt.

But in order to dig to another land

I needed something bigger than just my hands.

So I fetched Grandfather's shovel

and soon found a bit of trouble

in handling the cumbersome thing.

I could hardly lift it off the ground,

it wasn't that easy to swing.

Taller than I the shovel stood

and much heavier than I thought,

and when the shaft knocked my head

it kind of hurt a lot.

I remembered seeing a smaller shovel

next to it in the shed,

Grandma's garden trowel

she uses in her flowerbeds.

It did the job and my hole grew larger

until I hit hard ground.

The dirt was dark, and hard, and wet,

the earth was more packed down.

I poked, and prodded, and scraped about

but not much dirt from my hole came out.

So with two solid hands

and one big slam

I rammed the trowel down deep,

but all I did was bend the trowel's end

and that was all I did reap.

I figured Grandma wouldn't be happy

with how her little shovel now looked,

so off to the shed I trotted again

and took a hammer from a hook.

It was a heavy affair

to heave in the air

and drop on the trowel's tip.

And being in dirt

it didn't work

so to the nearest wall I skipped.

With a lot of hits

and flying brick bits

I was able to fix the tip.

And though it didn't exactly look the same

I hoped my grandmother wouldn't blame

me so I put it in the position I found it

so Grandma wouldn't think

that I had ever found it, and pounded it.

It was then when I turned to leave

that something scary occurred to me:

I was deep in the back of my grandparents' shed!

Then a scarier thought came to my head!

You see, the shed looks like

it was built

before the civil war,

with its mossy bricks covered in vines

and its thick old wooden door.

I wouldn't be surprised

if the shed was older

than the country in which it sat.

If America's over 240 years old,

I'm sure it's older than that.

And if that's the case,

came a pale tint to my face,

I thought of what might be inside 'er.

With all the cobwebs streaming about,

imagine the size of the spiders!

A 240-year-old spider must be quite large,

so out of the door I barged,

back to my sandbox, clear and free,

from all the shed's critters that could chomp into me.

Looking down at my growing pit

I imagined it going deeper,

but I wasn't about to go back in the shed

with all its slithering creatures.

In the kitchen I rummaged around

and pulled out drawers until I found

something that was hard and round

that I could dig with into the ground.

My search was rewarded with a large metal spoon,

and with that spoon I was digging soon.

But what happened next was that I bent that too!

With this digging thing, I was through!

The ground was too hard and forever it would take

to dig to another land,

so I thought of something else to make

as the bent spoon dropped from my hand.

A trap I'll build, for an animal to fall in!

Yes!

I'll catch him!

And tame him!

And keep him!

A tiger!

Cool!

No one will bother me in school!

I'll walk the halls in peace

holding my tiger at the end of a leash!

So I thought of the trap and what I needed -

a ground-covering of sorts,

like branches, and leaves, and twigs, and things -

and I set out on my course.

It just so happens that my grandparents' house

sits on the edge of a forest,

so into it I skipped without a path

for branches and leaves to forage.

I gathered some twigs but they were too small

and into my hole they all did fall.

So I tossed them out and set out again

to look for branches bigger,

I tried it again and this time it worked,

my hole the branches did cover.

As the tiger slinked

it would have to think

there wasn't a trap in the ground.

The tiger would have to notice nothing

even if it sniffed around.

Many armfuls of leaves and branches of trees

it took to cover the sandy floor,

and in the end a fine job I did,

my trap you could see no more.

Into the woods I snuck and hid

to wait for the beast to show.

Between two logs I crawled and slid,

but my impatience began to grow.

I heard no sounds

of snapping ground,

or a growl a tiger would make.

That was when

I realized then

I was making a big mistake.

To catch a tiger

it would be wiser

to have a bow and arrow in hand,

for tigers have been known to eat

women,

and children,

and man.

So I snuck around

and searched the ground

until I found a curved stick for a bow.

It took me more time

as it was harder to find

a straight stick to use for an arrow.

The American Indian used, I know,

some kind of thread from the wild,

some plant or such to string their bows,

but such a thing I couldn't compile.

So I snuck quietly into the house

and took a ball of Grandma's yarn;

I picked the greenest I could find

to camouflage the bow in my arms.

I strung a nice bow, I must admit,

but I didn't have any scissors,

so I rubbed the yarn across the bark of a tree

to separate one from the other.

The yarn stuck quite nicely on the tree's bark

and that's when a thought came like a spark:

What if the tiger escapes from the trap

and starts to run straight toward me?

I'm going to need something to catch the tiger

so it doesn't gore me.

What came to my head

was that I needed a web.

So with the rest of Grandma's yarn

I weaved so much in and out

it started to tire my arm.

But a thick web it was and if the tiger came at me

I would jump behind it,

and it would catch the tiger before it got me

and my web would tie and bind it.

All was ready and with my bow

behind my web I did stow,

waiting quietly for the tiger to come

until I thought, Well this is dumb.

Is a tiger just going to walk into my trap?

I think I'm going to need something more than that.

Something that might attract a tiger.

So back into the kitchen where I figured

that Grandpa's favorite snack I would pick.

A handful of his jerky would do the trick.

Back into the forest with another ball of yarn

where I tied many jerky charms

that hung like ornaments from the trees.

I tied them in a line so to my trap they would lead.

But when I was done I tripped and fell,

and let out of a bit of a yell,

as into my own trap I did fall!

And guess what?

It didn't cover me at all!

I got out of my trap as easily as could be

and figured a tiger could easily run free.

So back into the kitchen I thought of another plan

and returned to the yard with a big bowl in hand.

I know a tiger is just a big cat

and a big bowl of milk, he'd like that.

(Of course I added some cereal and had a few bites

to give me some energy to last into the night.)

In the middle of the shed I set the bowl down

and wiped away my footprints from the ground.

I didn't close the door but left it open instead

and went back to the house for more yarn that was red

that would be camouflaged by the brick of the shed.

I tied one end of the yarn to the rusty door handle

and back behind my tiger web I did scramble.

See, I risked my life to go back into that shed,

but the thought that was going on in my head

was that the ferocious tiger

would get in a fight with the giant spider

and the spider would bite him

and put its venom inside him

and put the tiger to sleep.

Then I would cage him

and tame him

until he was a pet I could keep.

With my bow in one hand and yarn in the other

I crouched in waiting for the tiger to discover

the line of jerky that led to the bowl,

and as it stood slurping I'd let out a howl

and pull the yarn as hard as I could

and it would slam the door shut!

Like this!

(I guess you could say it was a practice test.)

I got a little excited…

I must confess…

When I yanked on the yarn to slam the door

the yarn just snapped and fluttered to the floor.

If a tiger had been in there

it would have heard me for sure

and come running straight at me

with an angry roar!

Now after all this digging and hunting

I felt kind of tired,

so I went into the house,

slid behind the couch,

and there I did retire.

Next to the radiator that was warm and nice

because my cold hands and feet felt like ice.

I didn't wake up fully, I was still in a daze,

when I heard Grandma and Grandpa

talking in their soft little way.

'My yarn…' I heard Grandma say.

Something about it being all over the place.

'And cereal in the shed…?'

I thought I heard Grandpa scratching his head.

'The kitchen's a mess…'

'My jerky's hanging in the trees…'

'What's wrong with that child…?'

'Maybe it's mental unease…'

'I wonder where he his…?'

'We better go find him…'

And that was all I heard from them.

And then I fell asleep

and soon I was aware

that I had dug so deep

I was in China somewhere.

I was in a dark forest

full of ornaments

that sparkled green and red.

A big fur hat sat upon my head.

My leather clothes were all handmade.

I carried a bow made of solid jade.

Through this Christmas-like land

with reins in hand

I hunted a spider

riding my tiger.

The Lonely Cyclops

'I want to live in a world of unicorns and lollipops!'

This from the mouth of a little girl cyclops.

'I want to jump on a trampoline

and eat cake and ice cream!'

'We eat bones,' said Dad.

'Stop complaining, be glad.'

'I want to spin around in circles and dance!'

Her mom grunted, 'We're cyclops, we can't.'

'I want to have a birthday party

and invite all my friends!'

'You don't have friends, you're a cyclops, the end.'

'That's not fair,' the one-eyed daughter declared.

'You have one eye in the middle of your head,'

Mom said.

'You don't have a pair.

All we do with humans is give them a scare.'

Well, thought the young cyclops, this can't be so,

just because I have one eye, and large hairy toes,

and thick hairy arms, and a lumbering gait,

I shouldn't be stopped from having playdates.

There must be happiness somewhere out there,

and humans to play with, and games to share.

So away she skipped to search and roam

to find some friends to call her own.

To a playground she arrived. 'Wow! Hooray!

Look at all the children who want to play!'

'Ahhh!' yelled the children when they saw the monster.

'Hey?' asked the cyclops. 'What's the matter?'

'You're a one-eyed beast and you're going to eat us!'

'No I'm not. I'd rather eat lettuce!

I'm having a party, do you want to come?

I'll have refreshments and games, it'll be lots of fun!'

But the kids ran away before they heard,

along with the parents, the dogs, and the birds.

So the cyclops wandered all alone,

smelling spring flowers, and skipping stones.

The summers were full of shades of light

as the sun-filled shadows spun into night.

With her one large eye how beautiful it was

to see everything and all the world does.

She watched rushing rivers and their waterfalls,

and the wind rustling through the trees during fall.

She watched winter snowflakes drift upon the ground

landing softly without a sound.

But the fun she searched for couldn't be found

because there was never another human around.

Everyone scattered and ran away

when the one-eyed child came their way.

But still she wandered, and still she walked,

and to herself the cyclops talked.

'I wish I had a human to share

all the beauty for which I care.

I'd show my human the tallest trees,

I'd show my human the most colorful leaves,

I'd show my human the breeze on the ponds

rippling across the pink waters of dawn.

I'd show my human how the world comes alive

and blossoms into the stars at night.'

But alas there was not a friend to be.

Her cyclops looks just didn't agree

with all the human boys and girls

who had two eyes to see the world.

For years she traveled by herself

observing the world until she reached old health.

She wandered lands far and wide

until she came to an oceanside.

Down she sat and put her head in her hands

and looked at her hairy toes in the sand.

'This is it. I've reached the end.

I've lived my whole life without a friend.'

Her eye got red and started to well,

and from her eye

a teardrop fell.

A large teardrop it was

from an eye so big

that fell into a dead leaf of a fig.

But this tear, you know, it wasn't from sadness,

oh no, quite the opposite, it was from gladness!

She saw the world as a precious place

as ugly as she was with her one-eyed face.

And though she was a monster and made people flee

she chose to finish her life happily.

For she had something special, a gift if you will,

a special way to see the world.

She concluded right then and there

that she didn't need a human to share

all the things she saw in the world

during her life's Earthly tour.

For how would she tell a human, how could she explain,

what goes on within a cyclops brain?

It would be impossible, impossible to describe

what it's like to experience life

with one large eye.

So she accepted the fact that a cyclops she was,

and she accepted the fact of what a cyclops does.

Yes, she smiled, as another teardrop formed,

how lucky she was just to be born,

and that her adventures to find a friend

became something much bigger in the end:

She got to see the whole world wide

with one, large, glorious eye!

And what if my life were different

and I did have a human friend?

The cyclops thought about

how different her life would have been.

It would have been such a horrible waste

to use her beautiful eye in the middle of her face

to stare at the one thing humans like to see -

being stuck on a couch in front of a TV!

With that thought another teardrop fell

upon the other to cast a spell.

For the tide would rise and carry the tear-filled fig

to a little girl on a fishing rig.

A little girl who didn't like to fish,

working with her father was never her wish.

She didn't have any friends

because she fished night and day,

her only wish was to be with other kids and play.

But a poet she was and a poem she'd write

about a leaf she saw floating one night.

While most people wouldn't bother

to look at anything on the night's rippling waters,

the little girl had a special way

of admiring all the passing days.

Being without friends everyday on the sea

taught her to see things differently.

What she saw that quiet night

floating by her under the moon's full light

was not a rain-filled leaf but a giant eye

that winked at her when it passed by.

MEGAFAUNA!

Megafauna is what they'll be called

far in the future when I'm long gone.

If I were brave I might paint those scary things,

but who knows what kind of luck that would bring.

All I want to do is forget they're there,

so I paint things that don't give me a scare.

I can spend hours

painting flowers

and much more of

the megaflora.

Orchids, and cycads, moss, and ferns,

and other things in life that don't give my stomach a turn.

Camels and bison are okay too.

I'll paint anything

that doesn't want to make me its food.

If it were up to me all day I'd spend

painting on the walls of my cavern dens.

One good thing about living in the past

and not in the modern day,

is that I can paint whatever I want

on the walls of my home caves.

Maybe someday they might be found

deep in the underground,

uncovered after thousands of years

by one of your anthropological peers.

Although many days I have no wall

to paint my stories upon,

so I carve some wood, or draw in the mud,

before we're forced to move on.

With pieces of chalk

I draw on rocks

when I don't have a cave to live in.

With ochre or charcoal

my stories are told

on dried animal skins.

But if you ask me

my preference would be

to find a big cave

and forever I'd stay.

There's something wonderful about being hidden

inside of a cave with the protection it's giving.

I don't have to worry about being outside.

I don't have to worry about staying alive.

The caves we live in are always the best.

If it were my choice, I'd find just one,

and in it I'd nest.

I'd live there as long as I possibly could

painting in the safe glow of my firewood.

Imagine if I lived in the same place?

What a magnificent story I'd trace!

I'd cover every wall! Every cranny and nook!

With berries and haematite, I'd paint an entire book!

But here I am

collecting my stuff again.

For whatever reason

we're packing up and leaving.

What's wrong with the big people these days?

They always seem to have a craze

to head on out, pack up and go.

And it's scary out there, you know!

Every time we find a good spot

(as if the more comfortable I got)

and just when I'm about to draw a nice piece

the big people want to pick up and leave.

They give excuses like *water,* or *food,*

or something about the weather's mood.

Just as I'm feeling settled and warm,

'We have to leave right away!' they warn.

The old people often grunt at me,

'You're lucky to be a kid at this time!

When we were your age the land was covered in ice!'

And I think to myself, If that were so

I'd just carve a big house in the wall of snow!

Living in a cave of ice would be quite nice!

Think of all the cool things I could etch into the ice!

And not hitting the road

and staying in the same place.

But, no, it's always, *'We must go!'*

as if we were in a race.

Perhaps the nomadic life would be fine

and I'd have a good time

walking around

exploring different ground,

and I really wouldn't care,

and I wouldn't be scared...

But there's MEGAFAUNA out there!

Have you ever looked into the eyes

of a fierce saber-toothed cat

that looks at you as if with you

he's about to make himself fat?

I still have nightmares about the time in my past

when the big people forced me to take a bath

and sent me alone down to a river.

Thinking about it still makes me shiver,

and not because the water was freezing cold.

(Another reason why on taking a bath I'm not so sold.)

What still makes me wake up in fear

(besides the roar of some beast that's near)

is remembering when I sat on a log

to take off my fur shoes,

and suddenly I felt the log

start to throb and move.

I heard a rustle in the trees above me

and out slithered the head of a snake,

and then something stood up next to me

and started to rattle and shake!

As far as taking a bath

that one was my last.

And if I'm forced to take one again

I'm going to bring some friends.

I just don't get how my people survive

when our chances are so slim,

especially when we're all outside

without a cave to hide in.

How many times have we run into wolves

and our situation becomes more than dire?

Those things can chew through bones you know!

Thank goodness we invented fire!

The short-nosed bear?

What a scary beast!

As fast as a cheetah and loves to eat!

And like all the creatures it can hear quite well,

and let's not forget its sense of smell.

Which is why when we travel I stay downwind

from all the animals that danger can bring.

It's also why I wear a Woolly Mammoth coat,

a matted hairy hide that covers me head to toe.

I'm always told it smells

and that I'm the stinkiest in the clan,

but I'd rather smell like I do

than the tasty flesh of man.

So here we go again

and I hope we find a den.

A deep cave on a steep cliff side

where we can hunker down and hide.

Next to a spring

so we can have fresh water to bring.

Above us fields full of fruit and herbs

and below us a river of fish.

I just want a safe place to paint,

that's my only wish.

But what was that?

There's something in the brush!

The big people are telling us

to drop down and hush!

My heart is racing and I hide behind

the biggest person I can find!

The beast rumbles forth

and it gives us a surprise!

But it's only a giant sloth,

and we breathe relieving sighs.

And then,

sure enough,

we kill it and eat.

Sloth meat, I tell you,

is not a special treat.

And I won't be the only child

that in a couple months' time

will be saying, *'Sloth again?'*

with a groaning whine.

Large rodents, and giant bees,

fierce lions among the trees,

baboons, leopards, and grizzlies.

Where we're going to next who only knows

with tarantulas around my toes.

Ferocious boars and mean hyenas.

Everything just wants to eat ya!

I know one thing

when I get big

I'm going to find

a permanent place to hide.

A high-ceilinged cave with multiple caverns,

it'll even be equipped with an indoor bathroom!

And I'll find myself a sedentary mate

who also likes to be still and paint,

and we'll have children of our own

born with no desire to roam.

This wandering life, it's just not for me

and I don't understand, and I really can't see

who in their right mind would ever wanna

be out there in the world

with the MEGAFAUNA!

Sweet Dreams Tonight

When her baby sneezed

Annie claimed, 'Dear me!'

She spilled her tea

that scalded her knee

and caused her to jump

and make quite a thump!

This scared the dog

that frightened the hog

who rustled the cattle.

Oh, what a rattle!

A stampede, in fact,

with beasts rumbling forth

causing a ruckus throughout the forest!

Trees shook, the earth trembled,

and from the ground a dust storm assembled!

Blowing, and swooshing, and carrying on,

and on, and on, and on, and ON!

Through brush, and bramble, and desert nook

there wasn't a place the wind forsook!

Howling and spinning, hither and thither,

the town's people claimed,

'We're in for some weather!'

A cloud developed,

the sky grew dark,

then suddenly - *Flash!* - a mighty spark!

Crash boom bam!

Splitter splatter spew!

On and on the whirlwind flew!

And larger, yet, much larger than,

the entire bay of Galveston!

A hurricane it was,

a terrible tempest,

out in the ocean

being a menace!

Birds, and boats, and fish, and crew

around and 'round in circles they flew!

The storm carried on across the ocean,

the farthest lands felt its commotion.

A windmill spun,

a beret blew off,

a candle blew out in the Saint Sophia Mosque.

A reindeer bellowed,

a polar bear growled,

a wolf in Siberia let out a howl.

A potter in India,

a baker in Bangkok

both felt a breeze at eleven o'clock.

Whish whash whoosh

over China and Japan,

blowing the sails of a postal man

delivering a letter across the sea

to a woman in Texas named Annie McFee.

'Dear Annie,' the letter said,

'I'm wishing you well!

I miss our baby! I hope she's swell!'

With the letter was a picture

hand-painted for the child

of flowers and mountains

and a life that was wild.

Annie snuck into the room

quietly through the door.

The baby was sleeping,

hick, gurgle, snore.

She set the painting

on the sill

next to the crib

while all was still.

She closed the window,

turned off the light,

whispered, 'I love you.

Sweet dreams tonight.'

My Playground

It's a strange thing to grow up in the city.

I wouldn't exactly call it pretty.

Rusty fire hydrants, and tilted telephone poles,

trash on the ground, and the sidewalks have holes.

The artists who tend to paint on the walls

are the same ones who write on bathroom stalls.

Horns and sirens are always heard.

(Only in the morning might you hear a bird.)

Concrete, brick walls, and lots of pavement.

If trees are involved it's a slim arrangement.

But it just so happens it's where I'm growing up,

and like all the kids in the world, I just can't help it.

Which brings me to my playground,

the best part of my life,

it's where I like to spend my time

when I go outside.

It's where I play before school,

before I sit all day with a writing tool.

It's where I go when recess is called

and during lunchtime if nice weather is involved.

It's where I stay when school is done

waiting for my mom to come

to pick me up after she works.

(Having a single parent sometimes has its perks.)

I think my playground is a special place,

it's where I can play and feel most safe.

Although it's surrounded

by a tall chainlink fence,

and there's a turnstile for an entrance

made of thick rusty bars

that you have to push real hard,

and half of the playground is gravel and sand

where there should be grass covering the land,

and the other half is asphalt and tar,

I like it better than any park by far.

The very best time is when I'm the only one there,

when the playground is empty

and I don't have to share.

When all the equipment is just for me

and I can play on whatever I want, carefree.

Yes, that's my favorite time,

when the schoolyard is all mine.

When there's no one around

and it becomes my very own playground.

When it's empty, still and quiet,

without the students causing a riot.

During school days my playground can gather a crowd

with a bunch of kids who tend to be loud.

I'm not sure that waiting in line

just to use the slide is worth my time.

And sometimes I'll get stuck behind a bunch of beginners

as I hang in space from the ringers.

And if I'm on the merry-go-round with a crowded bunch

I'm taking a big chance that no one will lose their lunch.

But it's a very rare event to have the playground empty

and it takes a certain risk.

If I want it all for myself

I usually end up paying for it.

And I'm not talking about money,

I'm talking about my health and my time.

I have to go there on the hottest summer days

if I want it to be all ~~any~~ mine.

Lots of kids might call me nuts to spend a summer day

so close to school when most

want to be far away.

And I've heard a few adults inquire out loud,

'What's that crazy child doing

during a day that's hot and brewing

on that playground, running around,

on pavement so hot you can cook an egg on that ground?'

Yes, the heat in the summer

can be a bummer.

The playground metal gets so hot

that you have to rub your hands

with a bunch of sand

or it will burn like a red hot pot.

And even, still, at the end of the day

I'll end up with stinging blisters.

(Maybe someday I'll build a playground with shade,

and water fountains, and sprinkling misters.)

At my school all the equipment is made of metal,

except for the rubber on the swing

where my seat is supposed settle.

But the rubber is black

so if you sit down, in fact,

you get quite a burn,

so standing on the seat with both my feet

is the best way I have learned.

And pinched fingers in chains

can cause quite a pain.

The merry-go-round weighs a ton

but it's still a lot of fun

because once it gets going

it takes forever before slowing.

If the spinning starts making you sick

you have to risk your life

jumping off of it.

(I've come home with skinned knees before,

bruises, bumps, and multiple sores.)

If you climb to the top of the jungle gym

there's a chance you'll fall within.

Hitting your head on a metal bar

hurts about as much as falling on the tar.

If you're high up on the ringers

in the summer heat with sweaty fingers,

and your hand slips, and you find yourself in a fall,

it's a long way down, at least as far as I am tall.

And the sand isn't exactly a fun place to fall in

because there's a high probability fhere's broken glass within,

along with red ants, and goat's heads, and other things

that if you touch with your hand

they can cut you, or bite, or sting.

(Of course there are sunburns,

chapped lips, permanent squints, and dehydration concerns.)

But summer, yes, in the heat of day,

when no one else is willing to play,

when the ground seems to waver in the sweltering heat,

and no one is even out on the streets,

the place where I prefer to be

is where everything is just for me,

where I can do whatever I want

and nobody is there to tell me I can't.

Like launch from the swings,

or go backwards on the rings,

or run up the slide

and jump off of the other side.

Onto my merry-go-round spaceship I'll hop

and into outer space I'll take off!

I hope one day it'll happen again

and the hottest day I'll spend

running and playing and being forever free

in my playground

that was built just for me.

Too Much To Ask

Some things I'll never understand,

like when Mom commands me with an outstretched hand

to head my bottom right up the stairs

and take a bath and comb my hair.

Now I can see that by week's end

when the grime on my feet has thickened

and my clothes are splotched with clouds of dirt

and spills of food from the kitchen;

when after a summer's week of good, solid, hard play,

then I can see splashing off a bit

before I start the next week

the next day.

But this sudden decision of wanting me in the tub

to give my body a rub,

and get my body wet

with a terrycloth rag no less;

this spontaneous idea that I need a bath

right in the middle of the day?

This is something I'll never get,

not even when I'm old and gray.

So there I was staring

at my mother's outstretched forefinger

while the angrier she got

the longer I did linger.

So up I trudged

with a whiney grudge.

'I don't want to hear it!' she said. 'You're filthy!'

Through the bathroom door,

my clothes hit the floor,

and I turned the water to one hundred and fifty.

If I'm forced to take a bath in the middle of the day

then I'm going to have a say with its heat.

The hotter the better I was thinking

when something fell off the shelf and rolled to my feet.

It was a bright pink bottle with bubbly white letters,

Bubble Bath, it read.

Hmmm, I thought, *life just got better,*

as I grinned and nodded my head.

The bottle was new and hadn't been opened,

but I was adept at taking off lids,

from peanut butter jars to cookie containers,

so that's exactly what I did.

I was pretty certain (though I didn't read 'em)

of what the directions said:

I should use the whole bottle

if I want

bubbles up to my head.

So I poured it all in

and jumped on in

and put my hand to the spigot for more power.

Like my thumb to a hose

it's a trick I suppose

to make a harder shower.

This trick worked fine

because in no time

I had bubbles up to my nose.

But they didn't stop there

they grew in the air,

the bubbles rose, and they rose, and they rose.

It was fun for a bit to be covered by bubbles,

but I realized soon that I was in trouble.

I took my hand off the spigot

to stop making the bubbles grow,

but they didn't stop rising, the bubbles never slowed.

There's something about being in a nice warm tub,

even if it's your body you have to scrub,

and that something is being stationary and grounded.

What I was experiencing was something unfounded!

There were bubbles all around me,

I couldn't see a thing -

I was being pushed into the air

by a non-stop bubble spring!

Bubbles forever!

That's all there was!

Bubbles beside me, bubbles below me,

bubbles up above!

And they weren't just pushing me up,

they were pushing me all around,

and I was slipping and sliding in all kinds of positions

as there was no ground to be found!

I felt myself leaving the tub,

being pushed up to the ceiling;

I was wiggling and squirming—

I think I even took to squealing!

But none if it seemed to do any good -

the bubbles weren't popping

like normal bubbles should.

Larger and larger the bubbles kept growing

to the size of foursquare balls and exercise balls,

the bubbles never slowing.

I wildly grasped for something to hang onto

but there was nothing there,

all I did was slip and slide

through the bubbly air.

I spun and I twisted

this way and that,

backwards and forwards

like an acrobat.

Suddenly I was squeezed through bubbles

and flung across a floor.

But it was a floor of solid bubbles

and I could do no more

than slip and slide and fall down again

as I tried to get to my feet.

I tried and I tried but it did no good

and my falling I did repeat.

While floundering around on the bubbly ground

with a balance that couldn't be found,

I noticed a large bubbly figure sitting before me,

and at me he was looking down.

Now it wasn't easy to keep my focus

but I was sure as I could be

that the large bubbly figure was wearing a bubbly crown

sitting on a large bubbly seat.

As I slipped, and fell, and slipped, and fell

forwards, and backwards, and sideways,

he was shaking his head at me

with an angry gaze.

He wasn't the only one,

as I twisted, and as I spun,

there were large bubbly people, and tiny bubbly people,

floating in the air;

as I flipped, and dipped, and fell about

they gave me a similar stare.

Then I heard the bubbly voice

of the king that sat before me.

'This must b-b-be the little b-b-boy

who is always very d-d-dirty!'

Yes, it's true, that at that time

my skin had a bit of grime.

And, yes, it's true, that amidst the bubbles

my dirt had appeared to double.

I'm sure that you've been privy

to how lovely a bubble can be,

with its round body that glimmers and shines

in perfect symmetry.

It has no blood or bones holding it up from within,

only beautiful rainbows

skimming across its silky skin.

As far as being spotless,

and as far as cleanliness goes,

there's nothing cleaner than a bubble,

I suppose.

As I was sliding around,

as if in a room full of mirrors,

the gazillions of my reflections

made it to me quite clear

that I was the dirtiest thing they had ever seen

in this land of bubbles that was always clean.

I saw myself as I fell about

in the reflections being produced

of a dirty boy flailing around

and all the dirt I introduced.

Then suddenly - *Pop!* - and a round of gasps

from the bubbles all around me.

'That dirty child,' a bubble shouted,

'just popped my little Eddy!'

It's very true that the tiniest bit

of the tiniest bit of grit

applied to a delicate bubble's skin

can do a bubble in.

And as I tried to catch my balance on the slippery ground

I just happened to be, accidentally,

flinging my dirt around.

Pop! I heard, and then five more,

Pop! Pop! Pop! Pop! Pop!

'There go the Joneses!' the bubbles shouted.

'Make that child stop!'

'But—uh—um—*whoa!*'

I tried to say,

as I slipped away,

that it really wasn't my fault,

and if I could find an exit I'd surely go

before another one of them popped.

But as it stood

it was no good

because I couldn't even talk

as the soapy ground

spun me around,

much less try to walk!

Pop! Pop! Pop!

Pop! Pop! Pop!

'He's going to destroy us all!'

Pop! Pop! Pop!

Pop! Pop! Pop!

The king made a bellowing call.

'B-b-bring in the horses!

B-b-bring in the horses!

C-c-clean this child at once!'

Pop! Pop! Pop!

Pop! Pop! Pop!

'B-b-bring in the horses!

B-b-bring in the horses!

make his d-d-dirtiness stop!'

Pop! Pop! Pop!

Pop! Pop! Pop!

And as if the scene couldn't get worse,

I was getting hit with soapy spurts.

As I twirled around

to the popping sounds

soap got in my eyes,

and it stung so much

I had to keep them shut

or I would start to cry.

So I didn't see when the seahorses came

holding a cloth in their teeth,

and I didn't see them circle around me

to cover me complete.

They wrapped me up from head to toe

and they pushed me all around,

and then they lifted me into the air

off of the bubbly ground.

'I-i-into the ocean!' I heard the king say

although his voice was muffled.

I heard shouts of joy

and cries of *Hooray!*

from all the other bubbles.

Then suddenly I felt myself falling

and tumbling through the air!

Kerthunk! I hit the water

and drifted down to I-don't-know-where!

Sinking and sinking,

the heavy cloth was pulling me down!

'Help!' I shouted.

'Help I'm drowning!

And I don't want to drown!'

Then everything went bright

and I squinted into the light

as the towel was removed from my head.

There stood my mother

with one arm over the other

giving me a look of dread.

'What is it with you and taking a bath?

Why is it such a difficult task?

Your dirty clothes are spread all over the hall

and hanging over the door.

And look at all the water you've spilled

upon the bathroom floor.

The bottle of bubble bath is empty

and I just bought it the day before.

And your clean clothes look like

they've been abandoned,

can't you put them on the stand

where you're supposed to hang them?

Dirty handprints everywhere I see.

I just don't understand, and it's hard for me to believe,

how taking a bath can create such a mess.'

Her arms remained folded over her chest.

'And what's your towel doing in the bath?

How are you going to get yourself dry

after doing something like that?

And all the shouting,

and the screaming?

Baths should be a time of quiet.

But with you it sounds like you're having a battle,

a full-on water fight riot.'

She shook her head and at me she sighed

as if she were reviewing the facts.

'Can't you take a bath like a normal child?

Is that too much to ask?'

From The Desert

I was forced, I must say, to spend a vacation day

walking where I didn't think any person should stray.

I'm not sure what got into my folks

but when they told me of our vacation I thought it was a joke.

But the joke was on me

when I found myself on my feet

walking through a desert that was 110 degrees.

And that's no joke, it really was that hot.

Why my parents picked a desert vacation spot,

well, that's a joke I never got.

But there I was

with my head all abuzz

while the boiling desert

made faraway things look like fuzz.

And up close there really wasn't much to see

unless you like looking at small gnarled trees,

or you think a cactus is neat, or rocks are a treat,

or found solace in the sand that was melting my feet.

All these things for their beauty I just couldn't see,

but my parents thought it was the best place

they could ever be.

Which was quite discouraging

and I thought they might come to their senses

especially when we came upon rusty barbed-wire fences.

But did they turn around? No, they kept going.

When I ripped my skirt, all my mom said was,

'That'll need sewing.'

That's when it became obvious to me

we were going spend the entire day

in the desert heat.

For the first few hours I tried to see it their way

as they spoke of the great things we'd see that day.

They kept mentioning an oasis

but I didn't know that word

and they spoke of water and trees

but I thought it absurd.

I even stopped and said,

'Are you kidding me?

All I see is nothing!

That's all I see!

We could be swimming in the hotel pool!

Or watching television in a room that's cool!'

But they're adults with far away cares

and my complaint was met with impatient stares

and them saying again, 'We're almost there.'

But by that time,

I really didn't care.

I'd had enough of this horrible walk

and all the imaginary, fanciful talk

of pictures on rocks and dinosaur prints.

With this silly walk, I was done, that was it!

I stopped, and sat down, and said, 'I'm not walking anymore!'

and plopped myself on the trail, on the desert floor.

But they kept going and said,

'We're going to leave you behind

if all you're going to do is whine.'

'Fine!' I said, 'I don't care!

I'm not moving! I'm staying right here!'

And what do you think they did?

Do you think they listened to a word I said?

No! Of course not! They kept walking instead!

'We'll pick you up on the way back!'

they shouted over their daypacks.

'Just make sure you don't stray too far from the track!

And you might want to find some shade on the side of the trail,

and make sure no rattlesnakes or scorpions bite you on the tail!'

Rattlesnakes or scorpions? Well I stood up fast,

I didn't like the sound of that.

But I didn't move, I stood my ground,

all the while looking around

to see if there were any of those things coming after me.

But none of those creatures I could see.

What I did see, though, were my parents leaving me behind

which I thought was totally unfair in my mind.

They're going to leave their only child alone in the desert?

wondering if that would be something they'd later regret.

Although I do remember them saying

something about my day of complaining

which was probably why they weren't doing any waiting,

and why they didn't even turn around

and kept walking, faces to the ground.

Smaller and smaller they got until they disappeared.

I was so angry I shouted with some tears,

'Leave me here! I don't care!'

I yelled as loud as I could into the air.

But the desert air felt so thick

I don't think they heard a word of it.

What was done was done

and I thought I might run

as fast as I could to catch up with them.

But if I did, what then?

More hot walking?

And listening to their silly talking?

'Fine!' I said out loud. 'They'll see!'

What can happen when they let me be

all by myself, in the desert, all alone!

I can take care of myself

on my own!

So I found a small tree that was the only shade

and under its tiny canopy I made

I nice soft seat in the desert sand

that I pushed together with both of my hands.

And there I sat hiding from the sun

until I realized I was the only one.

All by myself, no one in sight,

and suddenly I had a terrible fright.

What if something happened

and my parents never returned,

and I'd have to sit here day after day

trying not to get burned?

They didn't even leave me with water!

Then I got mad at them again

thinking about what they were doing

to their only daughter.

I looked out into the distance that was so vast and grand

and thought how small I was in this bleak and barren land.

Everything was quiet and the air was hot and still,

even singing to myself the quiet air it didn't fill.

I looked around for scorpions, snakes, and spiders.

That's when I saw a bee buzzing inside a flower.

A beautiful flower of purple and blue,

and when I got closer I saw different hues

of oranges, and yellows, and a magenta red,

and the bee had the strangest eyes on its head.

Its coat looked like black and gold fur,

and when it left the flower its wings moved in a blur.

I watched it fly around for awhile

until it found another flower.

I guess I hadn't been looking closely enough at the desert floor

because the bee kept finding flowers I had never seen before.

I wondered how and where in the desert a bee might live

and thought it would be fun to follow it, so that's what I did.

It led me to flowers that I would have never seen,

including one growing out of a desert rock's seam.

And then the bee flew off super fast

and I couldn't keep up through all the cactus.

But while I was running something skittered past

that had me stopping dead in my tracks.

There was a big red rock and it ran behind it,

so I snuck up to the rock soft and quiet.

Slowly I looked around the rock

hoping the thing wouldn't run off.

First I saw its tail, and then its legs,

and then its whole body and its head turned sideways

as if he were listening to me sneak up on him.

That's when I saw his eyes and he knew I was upon him.

He looked at me and I looked at him

and while we were both frozen I took it all in.

He looked like a tiny dinosaur,

unlike anything I had been so close to before.

His eyes were yellow like a cat's

and had different layers that moved like slats,

like his eyes were made for extra protection,

probably from the sand that blew in his direction.

Long sharp claws curved off his feet and hands

that he used to climb straight up rocks with

was what I imagined.

He looked like he had been living forever as a desert reptile -

his skin was jagged, hard, and lumpy

like a crocodile's.

He had deep dark colors of purple, red, and blue

except his belly that was yellow—then off he flew!

Just like that so I ran too!

We both scrambled to the next rock,

but he zoomed past it to another crop.

I've never seen anything run so fast

and wondered if an alligator could run like that.

For if it could

then people should

take a few more precautions

before getting up close

just so they can boast

that they took a photo of a gator in action.

When I got to the rocks he just disappeared,

for I searched and I searched but he wasn't there.

That's when I heard a rumbling, or a growling, I wasn't sure.

So I stood real still to figure out

what it was that I just heard.

It came again. It was a rumbling like thunder.

But the sky was cloudless and blue so it made me wonder,

How could I be hearing a thunder sound?

while I looked far off all around.

That's when I saw it, above a canyon far away,

a very dark cloud and it was coming my way.

It looked like a giant jellyfish moving through the ocean

and it was coming toward me in super slow motion.

A black and purple jellyfish with tentacles of rain.

Then I heard the thunder again.

It was louder this time so I thought I'd count

after the lightning flashed in the jellyfish cloud.

Because I know that between seeing the flash

and hearing the thunder

I could count to a certain number

to tell how far off the storm might be

and how fast it might be coming upon me.

I saw a bolt of lightning and started to count,

"One thousand one. One thousand two…' I counted out loud.

When I got to ten the air rumbled

and it started to shake the ground,

so I calculated how long it took

between the flash and hearing the sound.

Between seeing the lightning and hearing the thunder

I counted to ten, so ten miles was my number.

Ten miles away? I thought. That's pretty far.

But the sky in the distance was getting more dark.

Another flash and I counted again,

this time I didn't make it to ten.

The lightning was only eight miles away,

and the dark cloud now covered the light of day.

I'm sure glad that I can read

because reading can help you when you're in need.

Before this vacation that we took

my parents made read a desert guide book.

I remember reading about a man in a flood

and all about what a desert flash flood was,

and how flash floods can happen when a desert is storming.

So I remembered what I read and heeded its warning.

Most of the day we'd been walking in a dry river bed

that looked like water would never flow there again,

so I looked for the highest ground

and ran up to its crest to look around.

Even if the rain is not upon you

a flash flood can still come through.

Even though it might be sunny

a flash flood can come suddenly.

I saw a cave on the side of a cliff

and ran up a steep slope to get to it.

The rain began to fall as I ran -

huge drops that landed with a thud in the sand.

It felt so good that I stopped my running

and turned my head up to the sky

and let the cool drops hit my face

while I closed my eyes.

That's when I felt the shaking ground

and heard a crashing waterfall sound!

I opened my eyes to see a muddy wall of water,

it had to be six feet high,

crashing down the riverbed

filling it from side to side!

It came from out of nowhere

down the dry riverbed that seconds ago was bare!

I sure was happy I was no longer down there

because even where I was, on the hill, where I was safe,

I was still scared.

I've never seen something so powerful and so strong

as that flash flood, with its wall of water, thundering along.

A red muddy slurry of rocks and debris,

bushes, and boulders, and old dead trees.

The flash flood took out everything in its path

and carried it with it as it blasted past!

Then a *Flash!* and a *Crash!* snapped me out of my dream

as the wall of cloud

that spilled to the ground

was headed straight toward me.

The drops came faster, and harder, and louder

and it felt like I was standing in a bathroom shower.

But it felt so refreshing that I didn't care

as I pulled back my wet hair.

The rain started to come down so hard

that I couldn't see very far,

and tiny rivers started to rush past my feet,

and my skirt, and my shirt, were so soaked they stuck to me.

Again the sky lit up bright

with a cracking sound and a flashing light!

I didn't even count to one

and decided right then that I better run

and get to the cave as fast as I could

even though the rain felt so good.

I ran, and slid, and slipped up the slope

to another flashing explosion even more close!

The slope was steep

and I had to use both hands with my feet

to pull myself through the red mud

that was getting sticky and deep.

With another flash and a booming crash

I rolled into the cave,

and I couldn't help to feel some relief

as if it were my life I just saved!

Dirty, and wet, and breathing hard

I pulled my legs into a ball,

and looked out upon the fabulous storm

behind a waterfall.

And just as fast as the thunderstorm came

it started to slow down.

Soon enough the sun was shining

upon the muddy ground.

When the rain stopped I left my cave

and walked to the river below

to look at all the damage done and watch the water flow.

The river was now a few trickling streams

sparkling through the red mud seams.

The sun once again shined bold and bright

and all the drops on the plants looked like diamond light.

It was as if everything in the desert

just took a nice cool bath,

and everything was saying, '*Ahhh*,'

as it dried off and relaxed.

And then I saw it,

and how impossible it was,

and I wondered how and from where

the little thing had come!

A toad, the tiniest of toads,

hopping in the wet sand!

I bent down and it wasn't scared

as it walked into my hand.

It was so tiny, about the size of a button,

and I felt its sticky toes

on my finger it was clutching.

It was so small and so cute and when I held it up to my face

we looked at each other with the same curious gaze.

'Hey little toad, how do you survive out here?' I asked,

as I softly took a finger and ran it across its back.

It must have really liked that

because it shut its eyes like a purring cat.

'Well look at that!' I heard from behind me.

'You found a spadefoot toad I believe!

It can live under the sand

in the harsh desert land

as it estivates in a membrane of moisture.

And it's a rare thing indeed

to find it out on its feet!'

my dad said, as both of my parents got closer.

I asked if I could keep it

and together my parents said, 'No.

It's better to leave wildlife

to wander around on its own.'

So I put down my hand

and I followed it through the sand

as it jumped into the newly made stream.

'It needs to collect water,'

said my father,

'to survive in an environment so extreme.'

My legs were red and so were my shoes,

and my shirt, and my skirt, were stained red too.

Back in the car,

as I gazed out upon the desert far,

I said quietly, 'I don't want to leave.'

The desert land

with its red sand,

and all that, before, I didn't understand

was now a part of me.

Mars

I always wanted to live on Mars.

I always wanted to fly to the stars.

And one day my fantasies all turned real

when I was eating a box of cereal.

It was a contest on the bottom of the box

that had a picture of Mars and a rocket launch.

I had to cut out the picture and send it in

with my name and address written in ink.

The problem was I had sisters and brothers,

and not to mention all the others,

who weren't very accepting of the fact

that I cut out the picture without much tact.

They weren't upset that I had taken the picture.

They weren't mad like I had figured.

They were mad because I had disfigured

and left a hole in the bottom of the box.

And for a while that was all the talk.

But I was the young'un

and used to the tonguin'

and soon all the chatter disappeared,

and they went back to gossiping about something else

in each others ears.

Well, time had passed and I had all but forgotten

about the contest on the cereal bottom

when one day a stretch limo to my house rolled up

while I was sitting on the steps petting my pup.

Two men got out with a woman in a dress

and continued on up my sidewalk steps

to stand right in front of me with smiling faces

and ask me kindly if I knew the Paces.

Chuck Pace to be exact

and that just happened to be me in fact.

So I told them so

and then came the row

when my family found out

what they were all about.

All were stunned

that the youngest son

won a contest that would send him

farther from the sun.

Well I was beaming

and my eyes were streaming

and I couldn't believe

I wasn't dreaming.

I won a contest to go to Mars!

That's nuts!

And then the butterflies

hit my gut,

wondering if it was such a good plan

to go to Mars in a rocket unmanned…

Just me…

Without any of my family…

By myself…

Not even a flight attendant would there to help.

But before I knew it I was on a plane

and the whirlwind trip was quite insane.

But not as insane as being zipped up in a suit

with a round glass helmet and puffy white boots,

and being strapped down tight in a cargo hold.

'Hang on!' was all I was told.

The ship began to rumble

and my body felt like it might crumble

as the force and all the pressure

made it hard to keep it together

as we shot into space at mach ten.

I looked out the window and that was when

I realized what I was doing was really real.

Why did Mom ever choose that cereal?

Maybe you know what it's like to be high up on things,

be it a roof, or the stairs, or the playground swings.

Or maybe you've hiked a mountain

or driven up one in a car.

It doesn't matter how high,

it doesn't matter how far.

The point is this:

You knew you were going to come back down!

Which was exactly what I was thinking

in the rumbling sound.

I was leaving Earth,

leaving the world.

And as it got smaller

and as it twirled,

as I went higher

while everything swirled;

as the roads, the towns, and the shiny cities

all began to look itty bitty;

and as the lakes and oceans got smaller behind me

I was suddenly overwhelmed

by an uncomfortable epiphany:

I was really leaving the ground

and I wasn't going to be coming back down!

And as I was leaving the solidity

of what I once called home

I began to feel

what it's like to be alone.

Ahead of me I looked at all the stars

wondering if maybe I could see Mars.

But all I saw were millions of lights

and nothing but a constant night.

And this is how it was for who knows how long

as my rocket, through space, drifted along.

I must confess

it wasn't like

all those spaces-movie scenes,

I couldn't hit hyperspace and have stars zoom past me

as I hit light speed.

No.

All the stars,

they never moved.

It was like I was on a motionless cruise.

For days, and days, and days, and days,

bored couldn't even describe my state.

And just as I was going cuckoo,

twiddling my thumbs, wondering what to do,

and just as I was about to lose my mind

in the endless night with no sense of time,

from out of the distance emerged a tiny red dot

that slowly got bigger the closer I got.

And just like Earth that I watched drift away,

slowly, so slowly, the planet came my way.

But unlike Earth whose surface is blue,

and green, and white under the yellow sun's hue,

I wasn't sure if it was in my head

but this planet couldn't have been more red.

Red rocks, and red sand, red rocks, and red sand…

I was questioning then

why I thought it would be so grand

to live on Mars

with all its red rocks and red sandbars.

I saw no greenery representing trees.

I saw no blues where water might be.

Red, I saw red, not even a white cloud in the sky.

Everything looked so barren and dry.

But as I drifted down onto that treeless ground

I saw something shiny as I looked down -

in the middle of nowhere, a round metal building.

My new home was what I was figuring.

Now, see, here's the thing,

I thought the contest that I did win

was going to have more people involved,

and I'd live in a city that had evolved

into the future as a megalopolis town

with flying scooters and robots walking around

delivering food whenever I asked

and taking care of every chore and task;

and I'd spend my days as if in a game that's 3D

chasing monsters with the finest weaponry;

and there'd be fun friends that I could race

with my own hovercraft setting the pace.

But as my rocket touched the ground,

and a red cloud of dust swirled around,

and the rocket's engines wound down to a halt,

and the doors clunked open with a jolt,

and the ramp cranked down and landed with a thud

onto what looked like a ground of frozen red mud,

I realized then that there were no other winners

of the contest I had won.

I was the only one.

And as I was thinking it would have been wiser

to have hired a cereal box

contest advisor,

and while I was pondering my dubious choice

my thoughts were broken by a mechanical voice.

'Welcome, Chucky,' the lady said,

'to your brand new home!

The one standing before you!

Your very own dome!'

Now I've never won anything before

and my family has always been a bit poor,

and I guess I should have been more excited,

or maybe elated, or at least delighted

to have a home I could call my own

and everything in it that I'd own,

but as I sat there hearing my breathing

a little scared was what I was feeling

about what this new life on Mars might bring,

wondering if it was going to be my thing.

I undid my seatbelt, and with my suitcase in hand,

poked my head out, and looked upon the land.

To the left of me I saw a red desert

that by the looks of it

went on forever.

When I looked to my right

I was given a fright

as coming my way

without delay

was a wall of dust the size of a mountain!

Even through my helmet I could hear it howling!

When the ground started quaking,

and the rocket started shaking,

I knew I had to make it to my front door

before I was taken!

Down the ramp I ran as fast as I could

but I'm not sure it did any good

because that wall of sand hit me

like a train carrying freight,

and I forgot about gravity and my lightness of weight!

Mathematics has never been my forte

but right then in my head something did say

that my weight on Mars was sixty-two percent less,

and in that moment of windy distress

sixty-two percent from seventy-two

meant in pounds I had lost a few.

I felt like I was floating with my twenty-eight pounds!

It didn't even feel like I was touching the ground!

But I grabbed the doorknob just in time

as the wind hit me with a furious whine.

It felt like an arctic blast,

and I was wondering how long my suit would last,

and if the sand particles would rip it to shreds.

My new life was quickly becoming

one of onerous dread.

I held on tight to both door and suitcase

with the sand blasting against my faceplate.

And you'd think that because it looks like a desert

it would be just as hot,

but the desert landscape is quite deceiving

for hot on Mars it's not.

Minus eighty is the average temperature on Mars

which could turn to ice

the antifreeze in cars.

I immediately felt the coldness through my suit

and my toes went numb in my moon boots.

As hard as I tried I just couldn't hold on

to my suitcase that was suddenly gone,

pulled out of my hand as if shot out of a cannon

and blown into the storm without ever landing.

I'm not exactly sure how I got into my dome,

I think the direction of the wind changed

and into it I was blown.

But I managed to slam the door shut

and flop on the floor,

relieved I didn't have to survive more of that storm.

And then I took a nap…

I needed it…

It felt like I had just accomplished an impossible trip.

And in the sound of the storm,

and as I drifted off to dream,

I never heard my rocket ship

launch off and leave.

Months have now passed

and, yes, I'm alone.

In my dune buggy

around Mars I have roamed.

I have found no others,

no future towns.

I'm actually the only living thing around.

No animals are here, bugs, or plants.

I've even sifted through the sand looking for ants.

I've come to discover that I'd rather be inside,

in my dome, where I can hide.

And even though driving my dune buggy

is awesomely fun,

I wish I was just a little bit

closer to the sun.

For if I go outside I must bundle in my thickest suit

for warmth, and comfort, and oxygen to boot.

And it's kind of a hassle, and it takes some time,

for there are zippers, and buttons, and snaps

I have to put together just right.

My suit must be put on with patience and care

or I might find myself out there

without any air.

And, yes, riding the dune buggy wherever I want

is a thrill, and exciting, as over hills I can launch

with its big tires that can bounce over rocks.

It sure beats going out for a walk.

But leaving my dome

is a dangerous thing

for I never know what the weather might bring.

Have you ever seen those dust devils swirling around?

Those small tubes of wind spinning dirt from the ground?

Well Mars has those.

Of course it has those!

But the dust devils here are the size of tornadoes!

And just as mean!

One day I was out

and one nearly took my machine!

With me in it!

Which makes me wonder why I could be such a nitwit

to think that I could just drive around Mars

and lazily gaze at its two moons

from my convertible dune buggy car.

It was the scariest thing I had ever been in

and I never, ever, want to do it again.

Dark red clouds started to form around me

as huge walls of sand shrunk my visual boundary.

I had to drive as fast as I could

while the wind blew me around like balsa wood!

It seems as if lately

when I go for a ride

the weather on Mars

wants to take my life.

And in fact, right now,

as I look out my window,

there's a nasty storm out there that howls and blows

with hurricane-force winds

so thick with sand I can't see a thing.

And I'm not sure who designed

this dome made of metal.

(I keep telling myself I should check it for leaks

if the dust ever settles.)

When it's being blasted with sand

it sounds like I'm living in a frying pan.

But, yes, I guess,

I'm happy with winning the contest.

And wondering what life on Mars is like

will now put my mind at rest.

And my dome home is kind of cool

and I'd be a fool

to say that living on Mars

isn't better than school.

And not having any parents

to boss me around

is something I could get use to

I have found.

And I can eat whatever I want -

I just tell the computer,

open the box,

and there it is

piping hot.

And my 3D printer gives me everything I need

like an Xbox and a PlayStation

on my movie screen-size TV.

(Speaking of movies

I've seen them all.

I have the selection

of the entire sky mall.)

But lately I've been spending my days

looking out the window

with a pining gaze

wondering if I can see through the thick sand's haze

the form of a rocket or some other ship

landing out there

that will take me on the trip

back to my beautiful planet

with all the fish and flowers that I took for granted.

I think once I'm back there

what I'd really like

is to go to the park with my family

and fly a kite.

And next time

I'll read the fine lines

of the contests on the cereal boxes,

and won't be in such a rush to win

while being overcome with gaming impulses.

And I'll make right certain,

and I'll know for sure,

exactly what I'll be in for…

Because…

right now…

on Mars…

I'm bored.

The Clouds

It was a day like any other day,

one full of never-ending play.

Which is how I like to fill my hours -

outside, under the sun, in the snow,

or in a downpour rain shower.

I always want to leave

my home whenever I feel the need.

I have to be outside running around,

my feet constantly leaving the ground.

They say I'm hyperactive, but that's not me.

I just want to be outside where I feel more free.

They say I'm claustrophobic,

that I have a fear of being confined,

that I have ADD, and ADHD,

and other things I can't define.

But to tell you the truth,

to sit and listen to the names they give me,

I just don't have the time.

Especially during the summer when school is out,

that's the best time to be running about.

Kick The Can, and Ditch 'Em,

Capture The Flag, and Sardines,

with all the neighborhood kids I can play

those games all day it seems.

Which is what I did all day,

running about,

playing games with my neighborhood friends

until I was quite worn out.

And I found myself on a neighbor's lawn,

all my friends had long been gone.

The sun was setting and I was alone,

weary and tired to the bone.

I flopped on my back, and looked up at the sky,

and watched the clouds as they went by.

Something I had never done,

for I am always on the run -

chasing this, or dodging that,

or stalking stealthily like a cat;

jumping a fence, or walking a wall,

focusing on my feet, trying not to fall.

But being still and looking at the sky

was something in my past

that had passed me by.

But there I was, on my back,

looking up at the sky in the nice cool grass.

The first thing I saw was Snoopy, I suppose,

or Goofy, or some other cartoon dog with a lump on his nose.

I watched the speed of the clouds passing by

that I wouldn't have noticed if I just glanced at the sky.

You have to be still to see the speed of the clouds,

something you can't do moving on the ground.

Have you ever tried to judge a cloud's speed

while running down the street?

It's impossible, it is, and more than that,

you can't see the clouds change from this to that.

But as I was on my back,

in a state that was quite relaxed,

I could see the clouds moving, but just barely,

and I could see their shapes changing, but just barely.

Which is why I wondered how it could have been

that the cartoon dog that I had just seen

completely disappeared.

The clouds must be moving faster

than they really appeared.

But they weren't.

They looked like they were standing still.

And now had different colors in their once white fill.

I stared at them again to see if I could see them change

and what I saw was something you'd see out on a range -

a roadrunner bird zipping by

even though it was just a cloud not moving in the sky.

Its beak was pointed out,

and its speed blew back its feather crown,

its legs spun in circles kicking dust up from the ground.

The feathers had an orange tint

from the sun that was starting to set.

That's when I noticed the colors

had changed in the fluff.

I saw reds, and pinks, and even purples,

and a dark blue solitary puff.

But just like the dog that didn't last

(and I don't know how this happened so fast)

when I looked back at the roadrunner bird

it had completely changed.

It was now one of those 1800's locomotive trains,

with a round engine and gears that were gray with a bit of black,

and puffs of smoke coming out of its stack.

That's when I realized I better get home

for the whites in the clouds were all but gone.

It felt like I had just come out of a dream.

I had lost track of time or so it seemed.

And just like that, the day was done.

But it sure was a lot of fun.

I felt as if the clouds just took my thoughts

and with the day went drifting off.

I just don't know why the days don't last

and why they seem to go by so fast.

Wasn't the sun just high in the sky?

And wasn't it just my friends and I

running around and playing games,

calling each other silly names?

I went to bed thinking that those clouds

just told me something but not out loud.

It was as if the clouds just taught me

how time can go by so fleetingly.

The clouds, they showed me, how time keeps going,

and just like the clouds

time changes

without me even knowing.

But maybe if I focus on the time going past

I can make time and the moments last.

For if time is like the clouds then isn't the summer too?

I woke up the next morning

and jumped out of bed,

and into the day I flew.

Made in the USA
Monee, IL
10 December 2024

71328444R00142